KNOCKING HER UP

A TEMPERANCE FALLS ROMANCE

LONDON HALE

KNOCKING *her* up

LONDON HALE

LONDON HALE

To us.
Becuase we're awesome.

chapter one

NO MATTER HOW hard I tried, I couldn't find an excuse strong enough to absolve me from sporting an erection at family dinner night. I'd say it was to be expected—I hadn't gotten my dick wet since I'd moved back to the island almost a year ago—but even that didn't hold up against the fact that I was carrying around some serious wood, with my mom just twenty feet away. There was something wrong with a man who couldn't control his Johnson around his mother.

But it wasn't my mom who was my problem. Wasn't her husband or my stepbrothers and their dates. I could spend time with any of them all day without an issue. No, my problem was specific and confined to one woman. All bets were off when I was around her, which was why I tried to avoid her at all costs. Family dinner night was not something I could skip though, which made me both a mama's boy and a masochist.

"How goes the firehouse, John?" Owen Collins, my stepbrother of the past five years or so, clapped a hand on my arm. Not my shoulder, which seemed to be a stretch for him to reach comfortably. A fact that made me feel oddly like a giant—sort of as if I didn't fit. Which I guess I didn't in this family.

"Good. Quiet lately, which is definitely good." I caught the glance and smile of Eric's girlfriend as she grabbed a bottle of water off the counter. Eric—the oldest of my stepbrothers—slid up behind her, rubbing a hand over her very pregnant belly, a move that made my heart catch for a second, made my mood sour even more. Not because of her, but because of what she represented. What she was giving Eric in a few months.

I sighed and cracked my neck, wishing the whole monthly family dinner requirement thing would die already. I shouldn't have to stay and torture myself to spend time with my new so-called family.

Growing up, it'd been my mom and me. My dad had passed away when I'd been barely old enough to know what death was, leaving a huge hole in both our lives. We'd been a two-person unit for almost two decades, but while enlisted and stationed halfway around the world, I'd gotten an email from my mom that she was dating the chief of police. A few months later, when I'd had enough leave to make it home, they'd married in a quiet ceremony at the marina.

Both had lost their former spouses and had spent a lot of years as single parents, so I'd been happy for my mom. Thrilled, really. She wouldn't be alone anymore, I'd actually have the family around me I'd always dreamed of, and Wade Collins had seemed like a good guy. What more could I want?

Not to be related to the one woman who'd turned my head in years might be nice, but I wasn't one to get greedy.

"Anything I can help with, Yvonne?" Emery—the reason for my perpetual hard-on, my foul mood, and every bit of my shame—walked across the great room to the bar-like kitchen counter that served as a divider between the spaces. Her long, dark hair shone like the waters of the lake surrounding us after dark, and a small smile tugged up her firm, plush lips. Perky tits, legs made for spreading, and an ass that could be any man's downfall—the woman was sex incarnate. But there was a softness to her, a kindness I so rarely saw from people. Emery was sweetness and seduction, sin and salvation, all wrapped up in the hottest fucking package I'd ever laid my eyes on. She was my biggest want, my only addiction.

She was also my sister, for all intents and purposes.

"Emmy." My mom's excitement was obvious in her tone, her grin spreading fast. Everyone loved Em. Including me…only in a different way than the rest of the room. "I didn't see you'd come in. Come talk to me—I heard you're working for that fancy rich guy trying to revamp the old mall. Mr. Huntley, right? Is he as handsome as everyone's been saying?"

Fuck. That was a conversation I could definitely skip. My temper flared, my gut burning as I thought about my little Em flirting with another man. Emotions I needed to push back down so no one noticed.

I turned toward Jackson—Owen's twin and the Collins brother who worked construction on the island. He'd hired me on quite a bit over the past year, giving me work when he got too busy to handle it all. My forty-eight on, forty-eight off schedule meant I had time to work another job, and my obsession with his sister meant I needed to. I had to keep busy.

Jackson seemed to be interested in something on the TV playing across the room. That was good. We could watch the local news while Em told my mom all about the rich, handsome guy she worked for. The one I'd trade places with in a heartbeat to get to spend more time with her without feeling like a fucking creeper.

"Almost finished at the old lighthouse?" I asked, hoping he could distract me.

Jackson turned my way, frowning. "Close, but I'm stuck on pause until the zoning for the B&B comes through. I'm also hoping Colin Huntley gets the zoning to rework the vacant mall property, though. That's a solid year's worth of work, minimum."

Motherfucker. Colin Huntley…again. I couldn't escape that name or his connection to my Em.

No, not my Em. My sister…sort of.

I needed to get my thoughts off her. "He's the guy who wants to turn the old stores into apartments and shit, right?"

Jackson nodded. "That's one of the goals, yeah. He wants to bring affordable housing options to the island, which I think we can all agree is needed. Well, except Em. She never had to fight for a deal on a place."

That was the truth. Houses on the island were hard to come by unless you wanted to build a minimansion up on the west coast. Apartments seemed to be even harder to find, a fact I knew well from my search after moving back home. The only thing that had saved my ass from camping out in the backyard was that I'd recently left the Marines. My landlord had retired from the Corps and had given me a break.

Emery, on the other hand, had apparently run into someone's father at the coffee shop one random Saturday and had a nice little cottage to rent on the fucking lake five minutes later. That was Emery, though—everything came up roses with her. She was the entire island's little sister, which only made the filthy thoughts of how I'd like to smack that round, pert ass a few times while bending her over my shitty kitchen table even worse.

I needed a drink—one that could maybe help soothe the beast inside me.

"I'm grabbing a beer. Want one?"

"Nah, I'm heading to the lighthouse to get some work done later." Jackson leaned a little closer and dropped his voice. "Besides, I promised Dad I'd stay sober for this dinner after what happened last month. I'm assuming you heard."

I almost chuckled at his answer, remembering the stories from the family dinner I'd been able to wiggle my way out of last month. Jackson and alcohol didn't mix—on that, the whole family could agree.

All the Collins brothers were good guys, really—almost as good as Emery. The three boys, all adopted, were a little on the wild side growing up, but they'd mostly settled down. Well, sort of. They worked hard, but they played hard, too. Owen was a paramedic working out of the fire station across the island from mine, his twin Jackson owned his own business, and Eric, the oldest, had become a cop like his old man. They probably never saw Emery—the only biological child of Wade and Grace Collins—as anything more than their sister. Of course, they'd had a lot more time with her than I had.

Emery was the youngest Collins child; a miracle baby who'd arrived not too long after the parents had adopted the boys. The children had grown up together. Me? I'd known of Emery as a kid, but she'd been too young for me to pay much attention to. I certainly paid attention now, though. Too much.

"You grabbing a beer?" Wade hollered at me from the kitchen, where he stood with his arm around my mom's waist. With Em at his side as well.

I focused hard on him, ignoring the feel of Emery's eyes on me. Not wanting to look directly at her…as if she were the sun. My sun. "Yeah. Want one?"

"Please. That'd be great, son."

Son. Fucking hell, the man called me son. And there I was, stroking my cock every night to thoughts of his little girl. I was going to hell for sure. If I wasn't already there.

Escaping quickly, I grabbed a beer from the refrigerator in the garage, taking a moment to open it and down a few gulps in the quiet of the empty space. Remembering the wedding that joined my family and the Collinses'. My relationship with Emery had started on that trip. She'd been this cute, young thing—a teenager at that point—and had seemed to take a liking to me. I'd agreed to be her pen pal while overseas, assuming she'd write me an email or two then get bored. Not so. The girl had written me weekly, sometimes more than once, and I'd gotten a kick out of her notes. She'd been my lifeline to the States, a constant source of laughter and light in some pretty dark days. Those letters were how I learned of her kindness, her sweetness. How I came to think of her as my sister even though we'd only officially met once. We'd bonded over our similar life goals— marriage, a big family, a life filled with love and roots and a shit-ton of kids running around.

It wasn't until I'd separated from the military and moved home that I'd learned of her sexiness. The little sister of Temperance Falls had grown up, and I'd nearly hit on her at the local dive bar my first night back. Hell…hit on her was too weak. I'd nearly propositioned her to ride my cock that night. No one could have blamed me—I'd been expecting Em to still be the young girl from the wedding for some fucked-up reason, not the bombshell who'd caught my eye and made my dick hard as stone. I hadn't recognized her when I'd run into her, had had no clue the chick across the bar I'd been eyeing was Emery.

I'd been dreaming of all the ways I could fuck the hottie with the long hair that would make her breasts bounce when she'd met my eyes and grinned. For one moment, I'd been ready to pounce. Ready to say fuck my adjustment period into real life and toss that girl in the back seat of my car for a little bumping and grinding.

Thank God I'd paused.

She'd rushed at me, throwing her arms around my neck even though I hadn't recognized her. Hugging me as she'd said she was so glad I was home, and why hadn't I emailed her to tell her I'd be back that night.

The woman had gone from potential sexual conquest to little sister in two-point-five seconds, and the loathing that followed—of myself, my thoughts and feelings toward her—had buried me in guilt. It'd been almost a year since that night, and still, I fought my attraction to her. Still had to remind myself that though she wanted kids as badly as I did, even though she was everything I had been looking for in a forever partner, I couldn't have her.

Unlike her adopted brothers, I struggled with seeing her as my sister. The step in front of the title didn't matter—I was expected to see her as family. I failed. Daily.

"You gonna offer me one?"

I nearly choked on my beer when Em's sweet voice met my ears. Fuck, I knew better than to be alone for long when she was in the area. Emery had an almost preternatural sense of when she could corner me, which was another reason I avoided family functions. I was afraid of what I'd do to her if we ended up alone.

"What do you want, Em?" I hated speaking to her so roughly, but I needed to keep my distance. It still hurt to see her slim shoulders collapse in, though. To watch her almost shrink into herself.

"I wanted to talk to you." She pulled the door to the house shut and took a step closer. Then another. Making me curl my hands into fists so I didn't yank her right up against me. "About something important."

The scent of her soft perfume teased me closer, the swirling in her hazel eyes captivating. Fuck, this was a bad idea. "We can't do this in there? In the living room?"

"No. We can't. Why do you always act like you can't wait to get away from me?"

Because I wanted to touch, to taste, to break every rule between siblings—even stepsiblings—and bury my face between her thighs. Not that I could ever tell her that.

"I don't always act like that." The lie sounded weak even to my own ears, so I sighed and took a step back. "What did you want to talk to me about?"

She narrowed her eyes, her bullshit meter probably pinging like a slot machine. The girl was too astute to fool, and she knew me too well. "The anniversary of my mom's death is coming up. And every year that goes by, I'm that much closer to the age she was when cancer took her."

"Em, no. That's not—"

"I've spoken to my gynecologist about it, and

we've agreed the best course of action is to be proactive."

I hated the way this all sounded, despised the fact that my Emery spoke about cancer as if it were nothing more than a paper cut. "Proactive?"

"Prophylactic ovary removal. Based on my mom's history, my doctor and I think it's best to have it done by the time I'm twenty-eight. At the very latest."

Her words might as well have been a kick to my gut. I wasn't a doctor by any stretch, but I knew what ovaries did and why she'd want to hang on to them. What she would lose by having them removed. "Jesus, Em. I'm sorry. What can I do?"

Em suddenly seemed nervous, licking her lips once and not meeting my eyes. So unlike her. "You know I've always wanted a big family."

Of course, I knew. How could I not? She'd sent me plenty of notes with her dreams all laid out— she wanted professional success, but personal was far more important to her. That meant a happy marriage, kids, and lots of family around her. Those had always been her priorities, so I nodded, totally understanding that much.

"My time's running out. I can always adopt—and I will, probably. Maybe after I've…met someone. After I've gotten married." She coughed, covering up the low growl I hurriedly choked back. Fuck me, I couldn't think about her marrying some douchebag. Luckily, she didn't give me a chance to speak, instead continuing down her trail of thoughts as I stewed about the idea of another man touching her.

"But I also want the chance to be pregnant."

Jesus Christ on a cracker, that meant sex. The woman of my dreams was talking about having sex with someone else. I shouldn't have to listen to this shit.

Emery, meanwhile, probably had no clue I was about to explode. "I know it's silly, but I think it'll make me feel a little closer to my mom, if we can share that experience. And I don't want to sit around and wait, hoping my future husband will suddenly come along."

Wait for…what? "I'm not following you."

"I'm ready to have a baby. Now. I *want* to have a baby now." She stood tall, chin up, shoulders back, and locked eyes with me. "And I'd like you to be the father."

Every molecule of air in the garage vanished, pulling my lungs tight and making it impossible to take a breath. "Excuse me?"

"Hear me out, okay?" Emery practically lunged toward me, grabbing my wrist. Making my heart stutter at the feel of her skin on mine. Fuck me, I was going to lose my mind. "I know this is…unusual with our family dynamic, but we're not related. Not really. Didn't even grow up together. And you're my best friend. Even if you have been a brooding asshole since you've been back." She gave me a glare, one I could only roll my eyes at. But then she grew serious again, her voice dropping. Her eyes sad as they stayed on mine. "I want to have a baby, but I don't want it with just anyone. And I can't think of a better man than you."

I couldn't think at all, couldn't process anything other than a single argument. The same one that had haunted me for the past year. "You're my sister."

"No. I'm not. I'm Eric, Owen, and Jackson's sister."

Technicality, but one I'd concede for the moment. "You're still a kid."

That definitely pissed her off if her scowl was any indication. "I'm almost twenty-five, which may be a kid to you, but I'm dealing with some pretty grown-up shit right now. I'm old enough to make decisions that affect the rest of my life, and I'm doing it."

"Your dad would kill me."

"You're scared of my dad?" Her laugh sounded an awful lot like a challenge, one I'd already been struggling not to accept. "If he's too much for you to handle, I can deal with him."

I wasn't afraid of Wade Collins, though. I respected him. I knew how hard he'd worked to raise his kids alone, had seen it firsthand a number of times through the years. The man was the epitome of a father—strong, brave, and always there. The idea of disappointing him didn't sit well with me. But neither did disappointing Emery.

Babies. She wanted babies. My babies. That meant she needed my seed, my sperm. My cock. I'd have to fuck her hard and deep, have to come inside that tight little body way more than once to get her pregnant. My dream…my idea of heaven. Lord have mercy, how could I say no?

How could I not?

"We can't do this, Em. I can't—" Jackson, Owen,

Eric, Wade, my mom—their pictures cycled through my mind, pulling me away. Blocking me from even thinking about what I actually wanted. "They'd hate me."

Emery inched closer, raising her hand to cup my cheek. Almost making me whimper at her soft touch. "No one could ever hate you, John. You're too good."

My mom's voice sounded from what seemed like miles away, calling everyone to the table. Dinner. We were at the Collinses' house for dinner. With our family. Which meant I needed to go back through that door and pretend little Emery Collins hadn't set my world completely on end.

"Em, I—"

"Just think about it, okay?" She backed up, leaving me alone. Walking away from me with a sad expression on her face. One that might as well have been a knife to my heart. "Do me that much."

I nodded, unable to speak again. Unable to think of anything else other than the desire to tell her yes and drag her back to my place so we could get started right away.

Unable to ignore the visions of disappointed family members still haunting me. There was no way I could help her, not without destroying the family my mom and Emery's dad had created. She was going to have to find another way.

chapter two

WET PANTIES WERE the last thing I needed while standing next to my boss. Couldn't be helped, though. Not when John was within a one-mile radius. He could be a dozen yards away, and my body shot straight into sex mode. Goose bumps, weak knees, hard nipples… and I'd already mentioned the state of my panties.

I probably should have been ashamed that the only man who'd ever gotten me going like that was technically—*technically*—my brother. Stepbrother, to be precise. Stepbrother who didn't come into the family until he was well into his twenties and out of the house—out of the *country*. Stepbrother who'd never even inhabited the same home, with the exception of ninety-minute family dinners once a month. But from the way John acted toward me, you'd think we'd shared a womb.

No. I knew brothers. Knew how rude and gross and overbearing they could be. How they loved to make my life hell just because. How they'd sneak their nasty, dirty socks in with my laundry to get out of doing theirs, or pile into the car and then lock the windows so I had to suffer through a tear-inducing dutch oven courtesy of all three of them.

Not even close to my relationship with John…or the relationship I wanted with him.

I shook those thoughts from my head as I followed my boss, Mr. Huntley, into the firehouse for our tour, stopping to shake hands with Dwayne Montgomery, the captain. I'd been anticipating this visit since I'd set it up with Lola, Mayor Briscoe's assistant. John worked forty-eight hours on, forty-eight hours off, and I *may* have had his schedule memorized. I also may have worked the visit so it fell on a day he'd be at the station. I was a glutton for punishment, but I couldn't help myself. If there was a chance to see John in his uniform, I'd take it.

"Thank you for giving us a tour," Mr. Huntley said, gesturing for Mayor Briscoe and me to go ahead of him. "I'm sure you've got plenty of other things to do, but I appreciate it nonetheless."

"Of course." Dwayne nodded, shooting me a wink. "Besides, when Little Emmy called and needed a favor for her first big job, I couldn't very well say no, could I?"

A string of obscenities exploded in my head, but I kept my outward composure for the sake of my job. My father's best friend or not, the captain deserved a swift kick in the ass. Yeah, he'd seen me grow up, but so what? It was damn difficult to try to make something of myself, to try to be seen as a professional, adult woman, when everyone and their dog referred to me as Little Emmy.

"She does seem to have a way of getting what she wants around here," Mr. Huntley said, glancing at me, his lips tipped up at the corners. "Which is fine by me. I need someone who knows the ropes in Temperance Falls."

"Well, that's definitely Emmy. I remember one time when she—"

I cleared my throat loudly, getting Dwayne's attention. "Are the firefighters ready for us? We wouldn't want to keep them waiting." I tried to keep my glare under wraps, but from Mr. Huntley's hushed laughter, apparently, I wasn't quite successful.

Dwayne chuckled but kept his mouth shut as he led us through a door to the garage, filled with two fire trucks and a dozen firefighters, all looking in our direction. It only took me five seconds to find John in the group, his height putting him inches above the others. Carelessly mussed dark blond hair stood this way and that, and eyes I knew to be bright blue scanned the room. God, I'd been right to schedule this when he was working, my mouth going dry at how hot he looked. Broad shoulders stretching his Temperance Falls Fire Department T-shirt, arms crossed over his chest, brow furrowed. Probably trying to figure out what the fuss was.

"Gentlemen!" Dwayne barked, startling me

enough to force my eyes away from John. Like I was a kid caught with her hand in the cookie jar. Then again, I didn't suppose it was acceptable behavior to look at your stepbrother like you wanted to strip down, climb him like a tree, and hop on for a ride. "Please welcome Mr. Colin Huntley, CEO of Huntley Group, Mayor Kate Briscoe, and someone we should all know, considering she's been running around the neighborhood her entire life, Miss Emery Collins, to the firehouse."

I didn't have time enough to give Dwayne a grateful look that he'd used my full name instead of my nickname because I was too entranced by John. His eyes shot straight to me as soon as Dwayne said my name, and all the air in the room promptly evaporated.

I hadn't seen him, hadn't talked to him, hadn't texted him—hadn't had any contact at all with him, in fact—since family dinner night last week. When I'd cornered him. When I'd dropped the bomb I'd been working up the nerve to ask since my first appointment with my gynecologist.

He stared at me for a brief moment, his jaw ticking, before clapping Riley Nash on the shoulder and stalking out of the room without a backward glance. My stomach crumpled, my heart actually aching over his dismissal. It wasn't only that he'd obviously made his choice not to help me fulfill what I so desperately wanted—a baby—but that he'd changed into someone I didn't even know anymore.

When I'd started writing him letters all those

years ago, I'd done it because I'd wanted to get to know the newest member of my family. But it'd quickly become something else entirely. The way we communicated was so freeing, the distance of letters and emails allowing me to be more myself than I could with anyone else. And it didn't take long to realize our interactions weren't sibling-like, as I'd assumed they'd be. There hadn't been anything romantic there either—not at first. Just friendship. Real and true friendship. One I feared I'd totally annihilated with my request.

Though, he hadn't been the same since he'd been back. He'd become my best friend while he'd been deployed, and then suddenly, on his first day back on the island, I was a leper he couldn't stand to be around.

That was fine. I'd decided over the past year that I wanted a baby, and I'd gone after that. And while my Plan A—a baby with John—was apparently no longer an option, I'd have to move on with Plan B. Just as soon as I figured out what that was.

———

The tour didn't take long, and John avoided the rest of it. I never saw his head over the others, never saw his eyes peering at me. That was just as well. I needed to figure out what the hell I was going to do now that it was obvious he had no interest in helping me. And attempting to do so while staring at the only person my body—or my heart—was interested in wasn't an easy feat. I didn't have time to pine over him or daydream about what might have been. My time was running out.

"Emery." Mr. Huntley pulled me aside as the mayor and Dwayne chatted while the firefighters dispersed. "Mayor Briscoe and I have a few things to discuss back at her office. You can cut out early."

"Okay." I nodded, glancing at my watch, relieved I wouldn't have to try to focus enough to get actual work done. Mr. Huntley was of the work hard, play hard philosophy, which sometimes made him a difficult man to work for. It also sometimes meant I got to cut out at two o'clock in the afternoon. "I'll double-check your schedule for tomorrow before I head home."

"Perfect. I'll call you later this evening to get the details."

Par for the course with him—a late-ish phone call to discuss the following day's schedule. I didn't mind—not for what he was paying me. Hell, he could come over at two a.m., and I'd serve him tea while we went over it if he wanted.

I said my goodbyes, once again thanking the captain for making the tour possible, and hurried toward the garage door that led outside. Eager to get home so I could nurse my wounded pride and bruised heart. Preferably with a pint of Chunky Monkey.

"Since when are suits your type?"

I startled, snapping my attention to the right where John was tucked into an alcove just off the door.

"Since…" I shook my head, trying to follow him, all the while attempting *not* to get swept up in his presence. "What?"

"The suit. Calling you later." His brows pinched together, his jaw tight. "I didn't think guys like that were your type."

I narrowed my eyes. What the hell was he getting at? Since when did he care at all about any of that? If I didn't know better, I'd say he was jealous, but he'd made it pretty damn clear he wanted nothing to do with me like that. And didn't want anything to do with my proposition. "I didn't think you gave much of a damn *who* my type was."

He planted his feet and crossed his arms, his jaw ticking once. "I don't."

If I weren't so pissed at him, I'd laugh. "Then I don't know why you stopped me from leaving. Or why you care whether or not Mr. Huntley is calling me later. Or why it should bother you at all if we're going to discuss business…or pleasure."

John always towered over me, but right then, he seemed even taller, his obvious anger adding another six inches to his stature, easy. "I thought you were smarter than to sleep with your boss."

He might as well have slapped me for how hard his words hit me. Especially coming from him—the one person who knew me better than anyone. And the fact that he thought he even had the *right* to give input on a part of my life he clearly had no desire to be involved in? If my boss weren't standing across the room, I would've shoved John in his stupid, oversized, caveman chest.

Clenching my hands into fists at my sides, I glared at him. "Nope, just a dumb kid."

I shoved past him, no longer interested in whatever he had to say. No longer interested in even being around him, too angry to see straight. How he elicited equal amounts of irritation and attraction in me, I'd never know.

He hissed out a curse at the same time he grabbed my wrist, pulling me to a stop. "Emery, wait. I didn't mean that the way it came out."

"Well, I'm not sure how else you could've meant it." I yanked my arm back, hating how much I loved his touch. Hating how even the most innocent caress lit up my body from the inside. I crossed my arms, attempting to hide my reaction to him. Attempting to shield myself in whatever way I could. "Look, I get it. You don't want any part of what I'm planning. You've made that perfectly clear, and that's fine. You were my first choice, but that doesn't mean you're my *only* choice. I've got other options."

He didn't need to know I hadn't yet found those other options, but I would. I would, because this was something I wanted. Desperately. And as much as I wanted it with him, I wanted it for myself equally.

John's entire body jerked as he blinked in clear astonishment. After a tense moment, he leaned forward, enunciating every syllable in a low, gritty voice. "You have *options*?"

That voice shouldn't have done things to me. Shouldn't have gotten my panties wet—or wetter, as it were. Shouldn't have made my nipples harden.

Shouldn't have made my heart race. But it did. It *so* did. And if I hung around for even another thirty seconds, he'd be able to tell.

"Yes," I said, turning to go. Needing to flee to safer ground. Needing to get as far away as I could from John and his brain-scrambling presence. "Or did you think my world revolved around only you?"

I didn't give him a chance to respond. Instead, I spun on my heel and hurried out of the firehouse and away from John. Away from the person I'd offered a permanent place in my life—one he'd proved he held little interest in.

After swinging by my office to grab my laptop, I sped home, pulling around the side of the oversized main house and to my picturesque cottage on the lake. On a normal day, I'd be smiling as I drove up to the tiny white house, complete with window boxes full of fresh flowers and a colorful welcome mat out front. It was mine, all mine—my own little piece of paradise. Any other day, I'd daydream as I walked inside. Letting my mind wander to what it'd be like to have John filling up my space, making the perfectly acceptable-sized cottage feel way too small.

But today, I blocked it out as I parked and walked inside, dropping my laptop next to the love seat. Mr. Huntley wouldn't be calling for several hours, which meant I had nothing waiting for me but a bubble bath with my name on it, a marathon of *The Office*, and as many pints of ice cream as I had in my freezer. Not the most adult thing I could do, but after the interaction I'd had with John, I deserved it.

Tonight, I'd allow myself to wallow in the what-could've-beens, but tomorrow… Tomorrow, I'd—

A two-by-four pounded against my front door, the entire outside wall shaking with the force. I froze in my path to the bathroom, head jerking toward the sound. My heartbeat broke into a sprint, my pulse fluttering in anticipation. There was only one person that could be. My brothers—demanding, overprotective oafs that they were—all had keys and used them at their leisure. My dad wouldn't come over without Yvonne, and she would never allow him to announce their presence like a…a demand. And that was exactly what it was. A demand in four quick raps. One that said, *Open this door right now, Emery Grace.*

With tentative steps, I inched my way toward the door. Paused with my fingers pressed against the cool wood, both anxious and terrified about what awaited me on the other side. But if John wanted to pick up where we left off, fine. I'd do it. And I wouldn't hold back. Not anymore.

Even though I'd known it was him, opening the door and seeing his imposing form filling the entire width of my doorway still managed to take my breath away. He rested his hands on either side of the doorframe, his head hanging between massive shoulders that blocked out nearly all the light behind him.

And then…oh, then, he lifted his head, his eyes locking with mine. The anger and frustration I'd been expecting. But the desire that was so plainly clear? That nearly made me fall on my ass, and his low, rough voice sent shock waves straight between my legs.

"How do we do this baby-making thing?"

chapter three

JOHN

I WAS GOING to hell. That was all there was to it—me and my greedy cock were going to get dragged to hell for what we were planning to do. But I had a feeling being with Emery would be worth every second of torture later.

"Dr. Goodman and I agreed that within the next year would be the most opportune time to start trying, make sure I have enough time to conceive before the surgery." She paced back and forth in front of the couch I sat on, talking fast, hands flying all over the place. She was nervous.

Fuck, so was I, but I was also trying to hold back. If I let go, truly let myself believe we were about to do what I knew we were about to do, I'd have her underneath me in a split second. Emery was being all adult and shit, talking about cycles and timing and sticks she peed on to know when she was fertile, but all I wanted to do was spread those legs I'd been drooling over for the past year and thrust deep. Preferably multiple times a day until I had fucked a baby into her.

"Huntley Group provides a very generous maternity leave package, so I'm not worried at all about money or time off once the baby comes…"

I sat back, watching her, my heart throbbing almost as much as my cock. She was adorably flustered. Maybe she thought I wasn't truly in this or that I'd walk away before we could get down to it—she seemed awfully set on trying to convince me. What she apparently didn't know was that I was fucking her. Tonight. I had to. After holding myself back for the past year, I'd released the beast inside me, and he wanted her. If I didn't get her naked, didn't steal a taste of that sweet pussy between those long legs, I'd talk myself out of ever doing it. We had to have sex tonight.

"I realize this is a life-changing decision, but it's one I haven't come to lightly. I want a baby, and I'm ready for one."

I palmed my cock, trying to relieve the ache being around her always incited. That only made me cringe as the dampness of my boxers reached my skin. The girl was talking about something to do with birthing plans and maternity leave. Meanwhile, I was fucking leaking for her. Anxious. Ready. Totally—

"I know being a single mom will be difficult, but I can handle it."

All my thoughts fell out of my head, and I focused solely on Emery. "What the fuck did you say?"

She froze, looking at me with wide eyes as if she'd forgotten I was still there. "Uh…I can handle being a single mom? You wouldn't need to be a part of the baby's life. I promise not to come after you for child support or…or involvement of any kind."

I leaned forward, my elbows resting on my knees. Weepy, achy cock almost forgotten. "You think I'm the kind of man who would get you pregnant and walk away?"

Talk about fucking something up. I'd been struggling for the past year because I wanted to fuck my stepsister through the floor, worried people would talk and it would destroy the only family I'd ever really been a part of. Meanwhile, she assumed I was some kind of abandoning piece of shit.

Total FUBAR.

She gave me a full-on glare—cocked hip, "are you shitting me with this" look, and everything. "With how you reacted to this whole thing, I assumed you wouldn't want to be involved…um, after." Her ire faded, her hand gesturing between us as if she didn't know how to deal with an *us*. But I did. I was ready to get all up in an *us*.

I rose to my feet slowly, prowling toward her. Fighting between my desire for her and my fury that she'd ever think such a thing about me. "I'm not a quitter, Emery Grace. Especially not when it comes to family."

"I know that—"

"No, you obviously don't." Fuck, she seemed so little as I loomed over her, as I bent slightly to bring myself as close as possible. "If we do this, if I'm going to lay you down and slide between those sexy-as-fuck legs of yours. If you're going to let me thrust deep inside the heaven of your pussy and take my seed to make a baby, then I'm in. All the way in. I won't walk away from my own child or the woman who granted me the gift of carrying him or her. Not ever."

Her eyes were so wide, so green today in the filtered light of her place. So beautiful. I couldn't resist her. I reached out, running a finger along her jaw. Tracing the edge of her ear as I whispered, "I can't believe you thought I'd be some deadbeat dad. If we do this, we do it together. If I get to make a baby with you, I want the whole thing. The fucking family. I want it all with you. Why would you think you would have to be alone in this?"

"Why wouldn't I? You haven't exactly been receptive to me since you've been back."

"You're right, I've been an ass. But it wasn't because of you, sweet girl. That was all on me and my issues."

Her angry little scowl fell, her entire face relaxing into a look that was softer, more tentative. More Emery. "And those issues are suddenly gone?"

"Not gone completely, but I'm tired of fighting them. I'm tired of not having you in my life."

"You've wanted me in your life?" She bit that bottom lip I'd been coveting, inching closer until her breasts pressed against my skin. "I thought you were going to tell me no."

"I could never tell you no." I palmed her cheek, leaning in farther. Needing a taste of those cocksucking lips like I needed air. "You're my Emery. No isn't in my vocabulary when it comes to you."

I ran a hand up her arm, brushing the side of her breast. Wanting to strip her naked but knowing we weren't quite there yet. I wasn't a patient man, but Em still had things to work through, so I fought to hold on to my control…even as I swept a thumb over her tight nipple. Good goddamn, I couldn't wait to suckle her as I fucked her sweet pussy.

Em hissed, arching her back slightly. Enough so I knew she liked my hands on her. "But you…you've barely spoken to me in the last year. I felt like I lost my best friend."

"Haven't wanted to talk."

She grabbed my arms, clinging to me when I went full palm on her tit. Closing her eyes for a second as her mouth fell open in a way that only made me want to do more. So hot. So fucking perfect, my Em.

"What have you wanted to do?" Her voice escaped as a whisper, barely loud enough to hear. As if she were afraid to ask. Luckily, I wasn't afraid to answer her honestly. Not anymore.

"Kiss those lips that haunt my dreams." I ran a thumb over her bottom lip, nearly groaning as she sighed at the contact. "Bite your neck and leave a mark so everyone knows you're mine. I've dreamed of you straddling my face so I could taste every inch of you, so I could hold on to your thighs as I tongued your clit and made you come over and over again. As

I lapped every fucking drop. Then, when you were all sloppy wet and ready for my cock, I'd throw you down and fuck you hard and deep, let you ride my cock until you couldn't see. That's what I've wanted to do since I came home, Em. That's why I've stayed away."

"Oh." Breathy and soft, her whispered word enticed me. As did how she gripped my arms tighter, digging her fingers into my flesh, and how she almost sagged against me.

I chuckled, cupping her head and running my fingers over her cheeks. "You've laid out your plans for us to have a baby together, and I'm telling you I'm in. Not part time, not hit it and quit it. I'm in all the way. Forever."

Her nervous swallow didn't escape my attention, nor did the way she seemed to look me over. Cataloging me. Her eyes stopping to stare below my collarbone. "Just like that?"

"Yep. You don't need options—you have me."

She ran a hand over my chest, almost an unconscious gesture, and my control snapped. I leaned down, needing a taste. Unable not to take a little. I pressed my lips to hers in what I assumed would be a sweet, simple kiss. But Emery wasn't on the same page, apparently. She opened her lips against mine and ran her tongue along my bottom lip. I grunted, delving into her mouth like a man possessed. Tangling tongues in a way that should have been illegal. She was my every want, my every wish and desire, all wrapped up in a package that made me fall to my knees and beg for more. And there was no fucking way I was letting her go.

Teasing, pulling away with little nips to her lip, I gave her a second to catch her breath and open her eyes before resting my forehead against hers. "So fucking sweet. Just like I knew you'd be." I stole a tiny kiss, keeping things calm for the moment because I had one more question. One more thing I needed her to clear up.

"So tell me," I said as I licked her taste off my lips and dropped one arm down to grip her waist and bring us closer. "When do we start practicing?"

chapter four

EMERY

PRACTICING? He wanted to know when we could start practicing, and I still had to get it through my head he actually said yes in the first place. And not yes, as in *I'll jerk off in a cup to make a baby with you.* But yes, as in *I want to do* everything *with you. Want to be here through it all.* I wanted that, too. God, did I want it, especially with him.

I didn't exactly have a whole lot of sexual experience—okay…any, really. That meant I wasn't sure if I should've been as wet as I was simply from the fact that he was all in.

And now he looked at me like I was something to eat—something to *devour*. I never thought he'd be sexier to me than he'd been standing there in my doorway, all gigantic man intent on making my dreams come true. But now? *This?* I wanted to climb on and never let go. Wanted to lick him up one side and down the other. Wanted to—

"Dirty fucking thoughts." With a groan, he wrapped his arms around me and hauled me up against him, one hand gripping my ass, the other cupping my neck. "I can tell by the flush on your chest you're turned on. Is your pussy wet, baby? Are you ready for me already? I can't wait to get between your legs. To lick every inch of that sweet pussy and feel you come on my tongue."

I opened my mouth to respond, but all that came out was a moan John caught between his lips as he crashed them to mine. As he slipped his tongue into my mouth and devoured me. While I hadn't been on the receiving end of a whole lot of kisses, I was certain I'd been doing it wrong my whole life, because the way he did it… God. It wasn't just an activity. It was an *experience*. He put his whole body into the way he kissed me, let me feel every inch of him. And there wasn't a doubt in my mind every single one of those inches wanted every bit of me.

John pressed me up against a wall and used the hand gripping my ass to tug me closer. To allow me to feel the massive erection between his legs. I couldn't do anything but throw my arms around his neck and wrap my legs around his waist, grinding myself against him. Wanting to alleviate that delicious ache in my pussy. The one that throbbed in time with his thrusts. I couldn't think when he did this. Couldn't think with his hands exploring me and his hard cock thrusting against me and his groans in my mouth.

Wondering what would happen next. Wondering what else he could possibly do to soak my panties.

How could I have gone twenty-four years without feeling this kind of connection? Now that I had, I never wanted it to end.

"I feel you grinding your little pussy on me, sweet girl." He pushed against me, a slow rock of his erection right where I ached for him. "Don't worry, baby. I know how to treat this pussy right. I'm going to slide nice and deep inside you, going to come so hard and fill you up. But that'll be after I give you everything else. After I make you come with my fingers and my mouth." His voice rumbled in my ear, so low and so deep, the near growl reverberated all the way down to my toes. Making me want to fall into him. Fall and never leave. He took my mouth in a kiss, slow… teasing. Quick flicks of his tongue followed by soft nips against my bottom lip. "Where do I get to fuck you for the first time, sweet Em?"

Oh shit. This was totally happening. Not in some far-off sense. Not during a vague someday. Today. *Now.* As terrified as that made me, especially with his gigantic cock rocking insistently between my legs, I wanted him with a desperation that should've been alarming. "Wait…I need to tell you something…"

"So talk, but make it quick. I need you naked so I can get my first taste of your pussy. Need it like a starving man needs a meal." John moved his lips to my neck, suckling on the sensitive skin. Sending goose bumps all over my flesh. "I've been starving for you for so long."

I moaned, letting my head drop to the side, allowing him more access while letting myself just *be* in the moment. This wild, amazing, wonderful moment where the best man I knew…the one I'd been halfway in love with for so long…actually wanted me back. And not just wanted me, but had been *starving* for me.

"Em?"

Right. I needed to talk. "Um, when you say practicing, do you mean…you know? Or just other stuff first?"

He chuckled, his breath fanning across my collarbones, making my nipples tighten. "Fuck, Em. You talk like you've never…" Lifting his head, he pulled back enough to stare at me, locking his eyes with mine, his eyebrows raised in question.

"Well, that's the thing…" I bit my lip before releasing it along with a pent-up breath. Now or never. "I kind of haven't."

John froze, his entire body going stiff under my roaming hands as he stared. And stared some more. "Haven't…what, exactly?"

"Um…everything? Well, most everything. There was that one guy who got to second base in college, but—"

He growled, closing his eyes as he shook his head. "I don't need the details."

"Right. Sorry. Well, bottom line is I haven't…" I tightened my legs around him, grinding my pussy against where he was still so hard for me, the move eliciting a full-body shudder—from both of us. I wanted nothing more than to keep going—keep pressing and rubbing until I finally reached that delicious peak teasing me. But this was important. "My brothers and dad haven't exactly made dating easy. In high school, all the guys were scared to get within a mile radius of the house. College wasn't much better since I lived at home. And by that time, I'd sort of already… I'd sort of already set my eyes on someone, and I didn't want anyone else. So, yeah…you'd be my first." The words tumbled out of my mouth, too many bottled-up emotions to try to siphon what and how much I told him.

John didn't say anything—hadn't even moved since I'd started this whole speech. God, what if he thought I didn't have enough experience for this? To still do this with me? What if he changed his mind? What if it was some kind of turn-off that he'd have to teach me everything? That he'd have to show me how to please him? Guys liked girls who were more experienced, didn't they? So they'd know exactly how to suck their cock and what kinds of fancy things to do during sex to make them lose their minds. I had no fancy things to pull from my arsenal. Hell, I had no *regular* things.

"Is…is that okay? I can… I mean, if you show me what you like, I can—"

"Fuck me," he said as he dropped his head to my shoulder. "I'm going to be the first man to taste this pussy? The first one to slide inside and make you come on his cock?" He pressed a soft kiss to my neck. Another to the corner of my mouth. "That's more than okay, sweet girl. It's a motherfucking wet dream. So long as I'm also the last."

I melted against him, all the tension I'd been holding evaporating with those few words from his lips. "You want that with me?"

"I want everything with you." He pressed me into the wall, rotating his hips in a slow grind against me. "And I still need to get you naked."

"What do you plan to do with me once I am?"

His chest rumbled with a groan, his gaze going dark as he stared at me. As he looked me up and down like he could undress me with his eyes alone. "I'm going to show you what you've been missing all this time."

Sweet Jesus, I couldn't wait. "The bedroom's down the hall."

Without a word, he spun around and carried me toward my bedroom, his fingers creeping toward my pussy until he cupped me from behind. I shuddered, pressing down on his seeking hand.

"The sooner we get you naked, the sooner I get my first taste of this."

God, just the thought of John's mouth between my legs was nearly enough to set me off. Nearly enough to have me coming all over him, even through our layers of clothes. I'd dreamt of that, had woken up countless times with John's image in my mind, his eyes peering up at me from between my legs. And now I'd feel it, would know exactly what it was like to have his lips on my pussy...his tongue stroking my clit.

It seemed he was in as big of a rush as I was, his long strides eating up the space as he carried me down the hall until we stood in my bedroom. He didn't even pause before he tossed me on the bed, pushed up my skirt, and yanked my panties to the side.

"Hang on to something, baby."

And then he descended on me. No lead-in. No buildup. No tentative steps for my John. Oh no. He wrapped his arms around my thighs, lifting me up toward his waiting mouth. And then, with one final flick of his eyes up to meet mine, he covered my entire pussy with his mouth and devoured me. Already so on the edge, I didn't even have time to enjoy the sensation of his tongue on my clit before I was in free fall, my back arched off the bed and his name a prayer on my lips.

"So quick, sweet girl?" He gave one last swipe through my slit, long and slow, the tip of his tongue flicking against my oversensitive clit. "Good. Now let's get you naked so I can lick you right. I haven't had nearly enough of you yet."

I could barely blink, could hardly make myself inhale and exhale, but I didn't need to do anything. John stripped me, yanking off each article of clothing until I lay bare before him, my body outstretched on white sheets. And then he stared, a clear war going on behind those eyes. He looked at me like he both wanted to drop to his knees and worship me, and also wanted to completely wreck me—work me until I could hardly breathe and then start all over again.

And the scary thing was, I wanted it all. "Do it. Whatever you want, John. Do everything to me."

"You're not ready for everything. Not yet." He bent down and sank his teeth into my inner thigh, hard enough to make me gasp and jerk against him. "But I'll get you there."

This time, when he put his mouth on me, he did it slowly. Languidly. Like he had all the time in the world. Like we weren't both aching to feel him fill me up. Like we weren't both ready to burst in anticipation. He caressed me with his lips and his hands and his tongue, not leaving a body part untouched. When he finally got to where I was so desperate and needy for him, so swollen and soaked, he gripped the backs of my thighs, pushed my legs up to my chest, and held me open.

"Gorgeous, so wet and pink for me." He ran one hand down my thigh to my pussy, spreading me wide and slipping his thumb inside. "I'm going to murder this pussy with my cock, baby. And you're going to love every second of it."

And then he made me see stars. He covered me with his mouth, his tongue fluttering against my clit. He licked and sucked and blew against me, eventually bringing his hand into play. And God, when he sank a thick finger inside me, followed by another, I could do nothing but press my head back into the pillows and groan, rocking my hips up toward his hand. Aching from the fullness already inside me, while at the same time yearning for more. Something bigger and deeper. *Him.*

"Want you inside me so bad. Want to feel you."

"Let me take care of you like a man should. Hang on to me and let me do you right before we get to the fucking, sweet girl."

When he curled his fingers inside me and suctioned on to my clit, I couldn't do anything but what he asked. I gripped his hair between my fingers and held him to me, grinding against his fluttering tongue as I came with a scream. As I arched and panted and begged to God for the feeling to never end.

If sex felt this good and we hadn't even gotten to the main event, I had no idea how I'd survive. But as John pulled away, his heated eyes connecting with mine from between my legs, his lips shiny from what he'd done to me, I knew I was about to find out.

chapter five

JOHN

I'D NEVER WANTED a woman as much as I wanted Emery. The look in her eyes as she smiled up at me, her pale skin completely on display, her sweet little pussy I'd finally gotten to make mine. All of it added up to a treat designed solely for me. The ultimate indulgence. And I was ready to gorge myself on her.

"You think you're ready for my cock now, sweet girl?" I palmed myself over my pants before finally unfastening my jeans. "I'm going to fill you up so good. Gonna make you take every drop when I come inside you."

Emery rolled onto her side, her tits shaking with the effort. Fucking tease. "I'm not ovulating yet, though."

"So?" I couldn't help the way my lips turned up

as she watched me strip, as she stared while I tugged my shirt over my head and pushed my pants down my legs, leaving my boxer briefs in place. For now. I ran my hand over my cock and shot her my best grin, adding a wink so she'd know I was egging her on. "I think it's the perfect time for a little deep dicking."

Her snorted laugh only made her that much hotter. "How can you make something like that sound sexy?" She lifted her leg, pointing her toes as if reaching for me. My girl shouldn't be making so much effort.

I grabbed her ankle and yanked her down the mattress. Brought her foot up to my lips and kissed the arch like a fucking gentleman. "Everything about you is sexy to me, even that adorable snort you do when you're trying not to laugh. Maybe it's a reflection you see."

Her smile softened, her muscles relaxing. "You're so sweet. But it's still not the right time for me to get pregnant. We don't have to…today."

"No, we don't." I nibbled up the length of her calf, crawling onto the mattress so I could keep moving over her body. "But I said we were going to practice, and I'm nothing if not thorough. We're going to have this sex thing mastered by the time you're fertile and ready to ride me for a chance at a baby."

Emery bit her lip, her smile pulling tight against her teeth, curling into herself. Making me grin with her apparent happiness. But that smile quickly turned into a yawn, and I pushed up to give her room to breathe.

"You tired, baby?"

She scrunched her nose. "A little. It's been a long week."

"A long week working for that suited-up jackass." I ran my hand up her arm until I cupped her cheek. "You work a lot, and he asks too much of you. This isn't the first time I've seen you yawning and looking exhausted since you started with him."

"I get paid very well to work that much." Em turned her head to kiss my palm, but I noticed her eyes darting to the clock on the nightstand. Noticed her sudden distraction. "And Mr. Huntley'll be calling tonight to go over his schedule for tomorrow."

Fucking Huntley. Why he felt the need to call her at all when she wasn't in the office was beyond me, but whatever. I'd be the one rubbing her feet as she talked to him. I'd be the one with my face in her pussy before she hung up. From now on, I was the man in her life. Not her fucking boss who assumed he owned her every hour of the day.

The thought of the man made my temper rage. "He always call you when you're off the clock?"

"I don't get paid hourly, which means I'm there whenever he needs me."

"I don't like it."

"What if I said I didn't like you running into burning buildings and risking your life?" Her sass— evidenced in her arched eyebrow and clipped words— was back in force. The girl had me. Sort of.

"You wouldn't ask me to quit. You like the uniform too much."

"You're right." She smiled softly again, running her hands up my arms. "And you wouldn't ask me to quit either, because you know how much I enjoy it."

Damn it, she tricked me with that one. Looking all sweet but going in for the kill on the argument. I should have known my disapproval wouldn't have changed her mind. She was stubborn, my Em. But I had one more card to play…

"I still don't like you working so much." I ran a hand over her belly, making sure the tips of my fingers brushed along the top of her pussy. Making sure to keep my face serious. "You're going to be so tired once I get my baby inside you."

Em brightened, every inch of her lighting up as if the thought of carrying a baby—my baby—made her happier than she'd ever been. I'd do anything to keep that look on her face, that joy in her soul. Anything at all.

"But you'll be here to help me." Her words came out tentative, almost nervous, and her eyes held questions she seemed afraid to ask. "Right?"

Oh hell, there was no fucking way my girl was going to doubt me. Not ever. I'd make sure of it with more than words, but words were what she needed right then.

"Goddamn right, I will. I'll make sure you've got everything you need." I pulled her against my chest and rolled us to the side, my need for her overridden by the way her eyes drooped. By the yawning she couldn't seem to control. Once she rested almost on top of me, I stroked a hand down her hair and tangled our legs together. "Why don't you take a nap, Em? You're so tired."

"But you're still so…" With another yawn, she slipped a hand between us, running a single finger along my leaking, aching cock. "Hard."

I chuckled against her neck, biting softly before pulling away to kiss her ear. "I've been hard for you for like a year, sweet girl. I can wait a few more hours."

She grumbled something, but with her pressed against my chest, I couldn't hear the words. That was fine—it only took a few minutes for her breathing to settle into a quiet rhythm, for her body to go limp. She needed her rest, and I needed to know she was safe in my arms.

I never wanted to let her go.

———

The golden light of a sunset burned my closed eyes, pulling me from sleep just as much as the painful ache in my balls. Emery was wrapped up in my arms, her face against my chest, her thigh thrown over my hip. Warm and open to me. Comfortable.

I wanted to be used for more than her comfort.

I slipped a hand between us, beneath the boxer briefs I wore, stroking my hard cock from base to tip, unable not to. Something about her all sleepy and snuggly spoke to me, made me want to protect her, while at the same time made me want to rut her biteable ass right through the mattress. Em was fire and ice, smart and sexy while still looking like the girl-next-door fantasy. And I needed her to be mine.

I kept my eyes on her pouty lips as my hand moved up my length. Kept my thoughts on what it would feel like to slide between them and fuck her pretty face. Would she take me deep? Would she gag trying to fit me in her mouth? I wasn't a small man in any sense, and she was such a tiny thing in comparison. A thought that shot depraved images right into my head. Pictures of all the ways I could give her pleasure, all the kinky-as-fuck positions I could twist her body into so I could watch her fall apart. I bit my lips and rubbed harder, so close already. Desperate to come on some part of her, to mark her.

On an upward stroke that almost made my eyes roll back in my head, Emery shifted enough for the backs of my fingers to pass over her pussy. Her very hot, very wet pussy. I bit my lip and groaned, going for another stroke. Loving her little mew of pleasure as I passed over her clit.

Needing to hear more of those before I even thought about finishing myself off.

I slipped down the mattress, using my body to keep her legs spread as I rolled her onto her back. She'd liked it when I ate her pussy earlier; I could only hope me waking her with my mouth on her clit wasn't going to be a problem. Truthfully, I hoped it made her scream my name so all her neighbors could hear, but we'd get to that. It might take me a few more times to learn where to touch, what strokes she liked. Exactly how much pressure to put on her clit to get that sort of reaction. I was willing to put in the work to learn. I'd always been an excellent student.

Emery shifted a little as I settled between her spread thighs, mumbling in her sleep. My beautiful girl looked so peaceful, so at rest. I'd have said I hated the thought of waking her up at all, but that would be a lie. I wanted her to get some sleep, but I also wanted her to grab hold of my hair and ride my face until she came.

The second want won.

I didn't go easy like some chump trying to tease her awake. I dove right in, spreading her pussy with my thumbs so I could wrap my lips around her clit. Sucking hard and deep the second I had her delicate skin in my hold. Something she seemed to enjoy once she was fully awake.

"God, John." She jerked and curled until her shoulders were off the bed and her abs were pulled tight. Her thighs clamped around my ears as her hands flew to my hair. Gripping. Yanking as she rocked her hips against my face and hissed plea after plea for more and harder.

Fuck yeah.

I gave her more, all right. More tongue, more fingers inside her pussy, more strokes to what definitely seemed to be her G-spot. She shook and writhed, trying to seek out the right amount of sensation to get hers. Using me exactly how I wanted her to. Making me want to come as she rocketed toward her own release.

"John, please. I'm gonna… I'm—" She moaned

loudly, holding me in place as her body shuddered with her release. As her pussy sucked my fingers in deeper and her moans turned more desperate. I licked up every drop of her release, teasing her through the long seconds of pleasure. Hanging on to her thighs to hold her against me as I rocked my hips into the mattress. I needed to come. Needed it like I needed air. Needed to be inside her even more.

But her phone rang from somewhere on the floor before I could get my turn.

"Shit," she said, throwing an arm over her face. "That's probably Mr. Huntley."

Motherfucking Huntley again. I bit down on one fleshy part of her pussy, enough to make her jolt a little. "Don't answer—you're busy."

"He pays me to make sure I'm not." With a groan, she rolled out of the bed, smiling when I tugged her down for a kiss. "This won't take long, then I can take care of you."

My cock didn't like having to be patient.

As Emery paced the bedroom, still completely naked, talking on the phone about appointments and calls, I watched. Lazily stroking myself. Unable to believe my luck even as I bit back my frustration. I loved her dedication, but I didn't feel her loyalty to the job was rewarded. Or maybe that was just me being protective of her. Maybe that was me being…jealous? I'd never felt jealous before—not about a girl I had a crush on or anyone I'd dated. But none of them was Emery. None of them wanted to make babies with me. That made her infinitely hotter, for sure, but also locked in a connection we'd been building for years through letters and emails. This girl had allowed me in her bed, was going to invite me into her body specifically to get pregnant with my baby. Something that made me even harder thinking about it.

I needed to get up before I jacked off right in front of her—needed to take care of her and prove I was more thoughtful than the jackass on the other end of the phone.

When Em had a long silent stretch, I got up and grabbed my pants before catching her attention. "You hungry?"

She shrugged, which sort of pissed me off. We'd missed dinner because of the pussy licking and nap, and now she was too busy on her call to get something. It was already late, getting close to sundown, which meant she needed to eat. Yet she was neglecting herself because of work. That wouldn't do. It was time for dinner.

"No, the call with the staffing agency got moved to ten, and the lawyer will be at your office at quarter after." Emery scribbled some notes down on the pad of paper next to her. "I'll need to meet the inspector at the mall at nine thirty, so I won't be available to be on the staffing call."

Didn't sound like she was getting off the phone too soon, which meant it was on me to take care of her.

With a kiss to her cheek, I headed for the kitchen, stopping to slip into my pants along the way but leaving them unfastened. Hopefully, I could get a little food into Emery during her call so we could get down to practicing afterward. I'd be happy to eat her pussy again—could do it for hours if she'd let me—especially as a lead-in to sex. Full-on, thrusting deep, stroking my cock into and out of her pussy sex. Yeah, that would be the perfect dessert. My cock liked that idea.

But when I reached the kitchen, the challenge standing in the way of me getting inside her pussy seemed a little harder to conquer. Emery didn't have much in her refrigerator or cupboards, something I'd have to change. I couldn't take care of her with a roll of cookie dough, a jar of olives, and some ice cream. Not really. She did have eggs, though, and a leftover salad with tomatoes, onion, and green pepper mixed in. I'd managed with less. Omelet, it was.

My phone rang as I cut the vegetables into bite-sized pieces. I didn't think anything of swiping to answer, even though the number didn't come up as a contact.

"This is John."

"John, we need you." The sound of my firehouse captain's harsh demand sent a chill up my spine. That could only mean one thing.

"Where's the fire?"

"No fire. There's a gas leak in the main running under Main Street, and we have to secure the area. I need more men than I have right now."

I stared down at the cutting board, trying to work through the thoughts in my head before I acted. Emery sat naked in the other room. Waiting for me.

But my job meant something to the community, gave me a place and a family where I'd had only my mom for so long. Hell, my own stepbrothers could be on Main Street for dinner or some shit.

Emery would have to wait.

"Give me twenty, and I'll be there."

"Thanks, John. I knew I could count on you."

I looked over the eggs I'd whipped and the vegetables softening in the pan, thinking of Emery. Of spending the night in her bed. Of spending the night inside her. I wanted her with the passion of a thousand suns, but people needed me. Possibly even our brothers.

"It's no problem."

I ended the call, contemplating. Wallowing a bit, to be honest. A few hours, and I could be back. Would be back. Emery and I had plans. No one knew we were finally coming together, and they wouldn't find out just yet. We could have a nice, private couple of days alone to learn each other in more physical ways as soon as I dealt with this gas line thing. No one could hate me for befouling the neighborhood princess today. I had work to do.

Five minutes later, I walked into the bedroom with an omelet and a glass of ice water. Emery glanced up from the desk in the corner, her eyes wide. She'd slipped on a fuzzy robe at some point, had hidden her body from me. A fact that made my job easier.

"I've got to get to work," I whispered as I set the plate down next to her. "Eat, though."

"One second, Mr. Huntley. Let me check that."

She pressed the mute button on her phone and set it down, frowning. "You're leaving?"

"Gas main break on Main Street. I need to grab my gear from the firehouse before heading over there for crowd control."

Her face tightened, her brows drawing down. "Are you coming back?"

Silly girl. "Of course." I leaned in for a kiss, one filled with promise. One I hoped gave her confidence in me and us. One that left her breathing hard when I finally released her lips. "You're mine now, Em. Nothing could stop me from being with you. Besides, we've got a baby to make."

"I wish you didn't have to go. I never got to…" She stared at my cock. Not glanced, not took a look and then let it go. No, she fucking stared. I'd never twitched so hard in my life.

"Later. I can handle this for now." I grabbed her hand and pressed it where her eyes were locked, wishing I could feel her skin on me. She gave me a squeeze before huffing a laugh, leaning her head back in a perfect invitation for another kiss. One I was happy to accept. Her lips moved with mine, my tongue meeting hers in soft, slow strokes. Apparently, it was my turn to be breathless when we broke apart. "Now quit staring at my cock before I hang up on your boss and throw your ass back in that bed."

Her glassy eyes held mine, and her teeth came down on her plump, pink bottom lip. "Sorry." She didn't look a damn bit sorry, but I let that go. "Thank you for dinner. Be safe for me. I'll see you soon?"

"Couple hours." After one last quick peck, I headed for the door. Already planning how to get through what needed to be done without tipping off the whole damn town that I'd had my face planted between Emery Collins' thighs. It was going to be a long night. "Eat, then rest. I want to see you relaxed when I get back. We've got baby making to practice."

chapter six

EMERY

AFTER TWENTY-TWO YEARS of living in a house filled with an overabundance of testosterone, I'd loved being on my own. Had loved buying useless throw pillows simply because they were pretty, painting my walls pink, and walking around in only my bra and panties if I wanted to. For two years, I'd reveled in my own space. Had blossomed in it.

And now, after mere hours with John, my perfect little cottage somehow felt incomplete. Maybe because he seemed to fit so seamlessly here. While, yes, he made the small-under-normal-circumstances house feel downright tiny, he'd looked so at home here with me. Especially in my bed.

God, my *bed*. And the wall. And…everything. The way he'd taken charge, owned my body as if he'd been the sole giver of my pleasure for as long as I'd been alive… It still made my knees weak, just remembering what he'd done to me. I'd had my fair share of dirty fantasies, and over the past couple years, they'd all starred him. Not a single one of those perfect dreams had compared to reality.

But even with the perfection that afternoon had held, I couldn't help worry from weighing me down. Funny how that happened when I had so much time to sit and do nothing but stew. Each second that ticked by on the clock was like a bullhorn. John had been gone for several hours—much longer than I'd anticipated. It wasn't like I could call him and ask why he was so late—not when he was no doubt surrounded by people he may not want to know about us yet.

The worry I tried not to give voice to, however, was if he *wasn't* at work, but instead had simply changed his mind about me…about us…about what we were doing. It'd all happened so fast I still had a hard time believing it was real. Especially when he wasn't here. When his arms weren't around me, his weight pressing me into the mattress. Didn't have his whispered words in my ear, so dirty and lovely and full of filthy promises. Didn't have—

A sharp knock sounded against my front door before it opened, John breezing through the doorway as if he owned the place, tossing his keys and a couple bags on the side table. He searched the room, his eyes heating as soon as his gaze landed on me. In three seconds, with a cursory scan of my body, he might as well have flipped my *on* switch. My nipples tightened, goose bumps breaking out over my skin, the throb starting between my legs…

"You always leave your door unlocked?"

"Huh?" I shook my head, trying to make sense of what he said. My body had overrun my mind, short-circuiting everything that wasn't a direct live wire to my pussy, and he was thinking about locks?

"I know you think this place is all sunshine and rainbows, Em, but I'm really going to need you to lock your doors. Especially when I'm not here."

I frowned, my brows drawing down even as my stomach fluttered over his concern. "How about a hello before you start with the orders?"

His long legs ate up the distance between us until he stood in front of me and leaned forward, bracing his hands on the couch cushions on either side of me. "Sorry. I worry about you. Hi, baby."

"Hi," I breathed, barely able to think with him so close, with his words fanning across my mouth. Aching to feel his lips pressed against mine. I glanced down at them, mine parting in response.

John's tongue peeked out, licking a soft trail along his bottom lip, before his mouth curved up in the corner. "I can see how much you want me to kiss you, sweet girl. How bad you want me to slide my tongue against yours and swallow all your little moans."

I did. I really, *really* did. "Then why don't you?"

He reached up, running his thumb over my bottom lip, the soft touch leaving me panting. "Because if I kiss you, I won't stop at your mouth."

Yes, please, and thank you. "That doesn't sound so bad to me…"

With a soft chuckle, he straightened to his full height, then crossed back to the side table to grab a paper bag with handles. "If I don't stop at your mouth, that means it's going to be hours and half a dozen orgasms before we come up for air. That omelet wasn't enough nourishment to give you the strength to deal with what I'm planning. I know it's late, but I picked up an order of eggplant parmesan from Nonno Pino's for you."

Was it possible to actually swoon your face off? I had half a mind to reach up and feel if all my features were still on mine, because John had brought his A game. Not only did he want to make sure I was nourished—for all the activities he'd apparently planned to engage in with me—but he'd also picked up my absolute favorite meal in the whole world.

"You didn't need to do that." I followed him into the small kitchen, trying not to smile as he plated part of the entree for me. "I'm not even hungry." My stomach belied my words, the traitorous organ rumbling even as the words came out of my mouth.

He raised an eyebrow. "Wanna try a different answer?"

"Okay, so I'm a little hungry. But I don't want to eat without you." I rested my hand on his forearm, needing to touch him, needing to be close to him. "Did you get something? You must be starving after working all night."

"I figured you'd be my dinner, sweet girl."

A flush worked its way through my entire body, all the fun parts lighting up with the memory of him waking me from my nap with his mouth on me. Lighting up and short-circuiting my brain, making my words come out jumbled. "Oh, well—but what… You can't just—"

"Eat." He slid the plate in front of me, then placed his hands against the counter on either side of me, blocking me in as he brushed a kiss across my neck. As he brought his body right up against mine. His very large, very hard body. One exceptionally hard part pressed against my ass, and I couldn't stop myself from pushing back against it. Desperate to finally feel it in my hands. In my body.

John groaned low in his throat then gripped my hip, stilling my movements. "I'm going to fuck you right here if you keep doing that, and while I'm sure you'd like it, I'd feel like an animal for taking you like that your first time. Now eat your food and stop worrying about me. I'm just happy to be home with you."

How he could turn me on so much with his presence, while at the same time making me melt with his words, I had no idea. But he was damn good at it.

I leaned back against his chest, tilting my head to stare up at him. "That's sweet." Pressing up on my tiptoes, I placed a kiss on his jaw, pleased when he helped me reach my destination by leaning down. "But you can't survive on air, John."

I grabbed a plate from the cupboard, then dished

up the rest of my meal for him. Nonno Pino's portions were ridiculous, and under normal circumstances, a single dinner could stretch for most of the week for me. Hopefully, the extras would be enough to satiate him.

John rested his chin on my shoulder, dropping a hand to my leg as he allowed his fingers to roam up my inner thigh. Not stopping until they toyed with the stretchy material of my sleep shorts. "I never said anything about eating air."

If he kept this up, I'd go up in flames. Just spontaneously combust right there in my kitchen. What the hell was he doing to me?

"Well, you can't survive on *that* either. Come and sit with me." I grabbed our plates and pushed back into John's chest, smiling when he huffed but stepped away and pulled out the chair at my small dining table for me. "Tell me about your night. How'd it go at work?"

He blew out an exhausted sigh as he settled into the seat next to mine. "Nothing exploded, and no one got hurt. The street's going to be blocked for a few days while they fill in and repave, but everything should be back to normal soon enough."

"Thank God. I hoped it hadn't escalated too much, but I got worried with how long you were gone." I pierced a bite with my fork, sliding it between my lips and moaning at the taste. "This is so good. I've been craving it all week. Did you know this was my favorite?"

He gripped the table, his entire body stiff. Like he was ready to go off. Like he was waiting for the green light from me to pounce. "I did," he said, his voice a low rumble. "And if it makes you moan like that, I'll buy it for you every night."

That wasn't the first time he'd mentioned being with me every night, but it'd always been in regards to the baby. What about me—us? Was there an us, or was he doing this to be a family man? I knew what I'd like…what I desperately wanted. But did he? "You planning to be here every night?"

"That's up to you." He took another bite, chewing before he continued. "We can stay here or at my apartment. Hell, we can find a new place together. Whatever you want."

A new place? *Together*? That meant permanence. Which I obviously should've gotten by his willingness to have a baby with me, but the baby was still just an idea at this point. Something intangible for the time being. Living together could happen anytime… *today*. "You…wanna live together?"

He frowned. "You're going to be pregnant with my baby. What kind of man would I be if I wasn't there to support you?" With a shake of his head, he waved his hand. "We can figure out the details later, but when I say I'm in this…I mean it. Wholly and completely."

"Support me when I'm pregnant, yes. But I'm not yet. It might take months."

"Plenty of time for practicing."

I rolled my eyes, but I couldn't stop my stomach from fluttering at the thought of practicing. Every part of me south of my brain wanted me to shut up and hop on, but I needed to make sure we were on the same page. I needed clarification. "I'm not talking about sex, John. I'm talking about living together and when you see that happening."

He'd scooped up the last bite of his dinner, but he paused with his fork in midair, his eyes set on mine. Then, very carefully, he placed the utensil on his plate and turned to me, giving me all of his attention. "I've written you at least a thousand letters and emails. I've read about your dreams, your life, your successes, and your failures. I've supported you through all of that even when I wasn't here, and you did the same for me. You know what I want, you know what I like, and you know how much family means to me." He turned in his chair and braced his elbows on his knees, bringing his face closer to mine. "We're a family, with or without a baby. I've spent the past year wishing I could get beyond my desire for you, but I can't, and I'm not going to try anymore. So if you want to waste time being apart so you can reach some sort of decision about me, I'll give you that. It took me long enough to see you for who you are to me. But, if you're ready? If you know how much we can mean to one another, then why wait?"

Wait? I didn't want to wait—*hadn't* wanted to wait. I'd been sure about him for a long damn time. I hadn't realized this want went both ways—we'd just dealt with it differently.

I set my fork down. Licked my lips as I tried not to stare at his. "So what you're saying is you want to start now."

A single, short nod. "Now."

I tried to bite back my smile, but I wasn't quite successful. Lifting my chin in the direction of the duffel bag he'd dropped on the side table, I asked, "Can I assume that black bag over there is because you're planning to stay the night?"

"I'm a Marine, baby—I come prepared. That bag is good for a night or a week. Whatever makes you happy."

God, the thought of John here with me for a week straight…his body moving over mine, under mine, *inside* mine… His fingers and mouth and cock all working to bring me pleasure? "We could do a lot of…practicing in a week."

His eyes flared, his stare growing heated. "Are you finished with your dinner?"

Who could think about food? "Yes."

"Good." He pushed back from the table, then scooped me up from my seat and carried me straight to the bedroom. "It's time to stop talking about practicing. I'm a doer, baby. It's time to do."

Excitement and nerves swirled in my stomach as a shudder racked my body. I was already turned on and ready to go, my panties wet and my nipples hard points against the front of my tank top. But somehow, even after only our couple of encounters, I knew John wouldn't rush things.

No, instead he placed me on the bed, stripped off my clothes, and rested his eyes on me, intent clear. Before I could even beg that he remove some of his clothes, that I could strip him like he'd done to me, he settled on top of me, inhaling my gasp between his lips when he ground his denim-covered erection against me.

"The things I want to do to you could get me arrested, but I'm going to do them all. And you're going to love every fucking second of it."

Of that, I had no doubt.

I moaned as he kissed me, as he slid his tongue against mine, so hungry for anything he gave me. So hungry for *everything*. "John…"

He hummed against my skin, brushing his lips over the corner of my mouth, my jaw, my neck, then flicked his tongue against my collarbone.

I couldn't do anything but arch against him, begging him without words to go lower. So much lower. But first… "I want to feel you. Let me feel you, please. Let me see."

"Greedy girl. How can I say no when you let me taste your sweetness?"

With one last kiss brushed over my skin, he pushed off me and stood, then reached back to yank off his shirt with little fanfare. My God, the man was a masterpiece of male perfection—all thick arms and broad shoulders and defined muscles, the barest sprinkling of hair covering his chest. I needed to feel the coarseness against my fingers, against my lips.

Unable to wait another second, I slipped off the bed to stand in front of him, my hands going to his chest. Solid muscle under heated flesh, the fast *thump-thump* of his heartbeat rapping against my fingertips telling me exactly how much this affected him. I brushed my fingers across his thick pecs, circling his flat nipples and eliciting a rumble from deep in his chest, before trailing them down over the hills and valleys of his abs to the defined cut of his hips.

I'd touched John before, of course. Had hugged him, rested my hand on his shoulder or forearm, had even felt his thick fingers work inside my body. But I'd never touched him like this. With purpose. With *intent*. And I didn't want to stop at his chest.

"Take me out, sweet girl. I'm yours to explore, and I've been dying to feel your fingers on my cock."

I swallowed down my nerves, wanting what he'd suggested with a desperation I hadn't been sure I could possess. Fingers shaking, I fumbled with the fastening of his jeans, popping the button before dragging the zipper past the massive bulge hidden behind denim. The thick root of his cock appeared as his jeans parted before his erection sprang free, thick and flushed and leaking at the tip. He'd gone commando. And sweet Lord, the man was packing. Though, based on every other part of him, that wasn't exactly a surprise. He put my one and only vibrator to shame. Made me worry how the hell we were going to fit together, which I knew was silly. Didn't make it any less overwhelming, though.

I traced a single finger down his length, brushing my thumb over the moisture gathered at the tip. Wrapped my fingers around his girth—or tried to. All the while I stared, transfixed by him, my lip caught between my teeth. Nerves getting the better of me. Nothing like going straight for the gold my first time.

"I'm going to make it good for you, baby. Gonna get you so sloppy wet, that beast will slide right inside. But first, I have work to do."

With efficient movements, he stripped off the rest of his clothes, then pushed me back on the bed, situating me so my legs hung off the side. I braced myself on my elbows, anxious to see what came next. Anxious to see how he'd fulfill his promise.

He dropped to his knees, his wide shoulders holding my legs apart, and then, as if that weren't enough to open me to him, he spread me with his thumbs, baring me completely. I'd always thought I'd be shy about this act, feel self-conscious or worried or awkward. But with the way John looked at me, hunger clearly written over every inch of his face, how could I feel anything but wanted? But desired? But *craved*?

"Been dreaming about eating this sweet pussy again all night. You've got me addicted to you already. Got me addicted to your taste and your little moans as you come on my tongue. Need to feel it again." He blew a sharp gust of air straight against my already swollen clit, causing my head to drop back between my shoulders at the same time I lifted my hips from the bed, seeking his mouth. His tongue. But this was John's show, and he proved it by bracing his hands on my hips, his thumbs still spreading my lips apart, holding me in place for his torture.

"Please, John. Please, please, please."

"Please what? Tell me what you want."

I blushed, a thousand thoughts running through

my head. But I couldn't *say* them. Couldn't put them to words like he could. He could probably bring me to orgasm just from his dirty talk, but if I tried that, I'd no doubt sound like a star in a low-budget porno.

"Please what, baby?"

"Please…use your mouth."

"I am." Again, he blew against me, making me throb in want.

Groaning, I tried to lift my hips again to no avail. He'd gotten me on a damn technicality. "Your *tongue*. Use your tongue."

I sagged with relief when he lowered his head, brought his mouth closer to me. Then nearly cried when he flicked his tongue nowhere near my clit. Nowhere near where I wanted him. Where I *needed* him. He licked a path up one side of the crease where my leg met my body, then switched to the other. Frustrated, I reached down and gripped his hair, trying to guide him toward my clit.

"I'm going to need to hear the words from you, baby. I'll do anything you tell me to, but you'd better be damned specific."

"Oh my God, lick my clit. Please, John, please."

With a groan, he did exactly that, sucking me straight into his mouth before flicking his tongue over me. The direct contact after so much teasing had me seeing stars from the first brush of his lips against my clit. Had me arching off the bed with a scream before he'd even gotten started.

"That's one."

As I lay there panting, trying to remember how

to breathe, he swirled his tongue all over my pussy, careful to avoid my oversensitive clit. Then he added his fingers, those thick digits slipping inside me, one after another after another until he'd stretched me so full, I thought I'd die.

"You're going to strangle my cock in this little pussy, aren't you? So soft and wet, but tight. I'll never want to leave it. Never want to stop fucking you once I get inside. Gonna fill this pussy up with my cock until you drain me dry—until we've got a baby planted in that belly."

His fingers were no match for what hung long and thick between his legs, and I ached for that. Ached to feel him stretching me. Ached to feel him lying on top of me as he thrust inside. As he filled me with his seed.

The thought of him losing his mind inside me sent me over the edge again, John's fingers pressing deep and his tongue once again swirling around my clit. When the last pulse echoed through my body, I collapsed against the bed, my fingers releasing their hold on his hair, hands falling to my sides. Boneless. Sated.

"Catch your breath, baby. We're only getting started."

chapter seven

JOHN

MINE.

The word repeated through my mind as I looked up Emery's body. Legs bent, knees spread, she smiled at me with a confidence that stole my breath. So fucking gorgeous, my girl. So amazing.

Unable to hold myself back, I kissed a path up Emery's hip. She was mine to kiss, to touch, to fuck… to love. I was going to take my time tonight, was going to make things good for her first time. But I wasn't kidding about practicing—by the time her little body was ready to carry a baby, I'd be fucking this girl how I wanted. How I knew we'd both enjoy. Hard, fast, twisted into positions that put pressure on her clit so she could come quickly, with me pounding deep inside her pussy. All so I could get my seed in her. The primal urge to give her a baby too strong to resist.

"John." Emery's whiny moan as I licked a path to her belly button only made me smirk. She was definitely a needy little thing, which made me feel like a man. Like a protector. I wanted to be needed, wanted to know my woman enjoyed everything I did to her body and craved more. I'd give it to her. I'd tease her all night if she asked.

Hell, I'd do it if she didn't.

"Yes, sweet girl?" I slid my hands up her thighs, nudging her to spread a little more. To shift until my hips could fit between. Inching my way up her body toward her strawberry-tipped breasts.

"I'm ready. I wanna feel you inside me."

"I know you do. But I'm having fun." I groaned when I finally reached my destination. Her breasts were so plump and firm. I'd had dreams about them, had fought touching them for months. I wasn't fighting anymore. I licked my way up one soft, full tit, circling her nipple but not touching the hard tip. Teasing her. Watching as she writhed and frowned and tried to move me into the position she wanted me.

Not happening.

"Do you have any idea how many times I've thought about fucking your tits since I've been back?"

I leaned up on my elbow, massaging one breast while rubbing my thumb back and forth across her nipple. Emery had gone still, the only sound her heavy breathing. Her eyes locked on mine, dark and filled with lust. Apparently, titty-fucking was something she was open to. Interesting.

But she hadn't answered me, so I flicked her nipple. "Do you?"

Emery jumped and moaned, her head tipping back and her knees coming up to squeeze me along my ribs. "No. Tell me."

Good girl. "Every fucking day. That fantasy was usually the one I gave myself over to in the shower." I licked up her breast again, this time laving across her nipple. Sucking on it enough to get her moaning. "I'd soap up my cock and think of you kneeling before me, think of you looking up at me with those big, hazel eyes. Would they be more green that day, or brown? I never knew, but your tits would be full and ready, your little hands holding them together so my cock could have a nice, tight home. I'd slide between them, the tip of my cock moving up your sternum with every push while you tried to lick the tip."

Her nails bit into my back, dragging a hiss from between my lips. I had her worked up, had her clinging to me, digging her heels into my ass and trying to pull me where she wanted me. But not yet.

"Would you let me do that someday, sweet girl?" I suckled her nipple, pulling it between my teeth as I slid three fingers between her breasts and moved them up and down at a maddeningly slow pace. "Would you push these pretty tits together and let me fuck them? Use your body to please me until I came all over that pretty face?"

"Anything, John. I'd do anything with you— *every*thing."

I groaned, rocking my hips into hers as I gripped

and sucked on her breasts. So soft, so fucking perfect. Em wrapped her body around mine, pulling me closer, hanging on to me by my hair so she could try to direct me. Tugging to the point of pain, which only made my cock harder. I used to think I should shave my hair off into the Marine high and tight, but so long as my woman used it to get her pleasure? I'd wear that shit as long as she wanted.

"Need to feel you. *Please*."

Yeah, she wasn't talking about my hair right then.

"Gonna fill you up," I mumbled, the actions of talking and kissing running together until my words were little more than a murmur against her flesh. "Gonna work this pussy over until I can slide in all the way, until you can take every inch of me and love it. Then I'm going to come inside you. Keep you dripping with my seed until we make a baby. Is that what you want, sweet girl? You want me to fill you until you don't have room for another drop?"

"Oh my God, *yes*."

Fuck, I couldn't wait another second. As much as I wanted to get her off again, I needed to be inside her. Needed to cure the ache in my cock. I claimed her mouth in a strong kiss, groaning as she opened to me immediately. I slid my hand down her body and between her legs. So fucking wet. So hot. There'd be no long, drawn-out fucking tonight. Not with how wound up I was for this girl. Not the first time, at least.

My hand hit wet cotton beneath her, and I groaned loud and long as my hips responded of their own volition. Seeking her warmth.

"You're so wet for me, you're soaking the sheets." I notched my cock at her entrance, holding myself in place as I rubbed my thumb over her clit. "Can't wait until it's my come leaking out of you."

"No more teasing." She curved into me, forcing me another inch inside of her, and I gave up all control. I thrust once, twice. Seesawing my way inside, capturing her whimper in my mouth and rubbing her clit with my thumb to keep her focused on the pleasure instead of any pain. I couldn't remember if I'd ever been with a virgin, but I'd heard enough stories. I knew it might not be pleasant for her at first. I'd have to fight my instincts. Have to hold still until she gave me some sort of signal she wanted more, no matter how hard I was to fuck her. I needed to—

"Oh *God*. I didn't know—nothing's ever…" She tightened her legs around me and tilted her hips. My cock slipped in a little more, my body following hers, and she moaned as if my being inside her was the best fucking thing she'd ever felt. "It's so good."

Signal received. I pulled out slowly, thrusting deep again and twisting my hips against hers. Emery groaned, her hands shaking on my arms, her legs squeezing around my waist. Holding me to her. Fuck, this wasn't what I'd expected from a virgin at all. She seemed to like what I was doing to her, seemed to want more and harder and faster, which was good. Because I wasn't stopping unless she told me to.

"Can't fucking believe you're so tight," I mumbled. "Want to feel you come on my cock, sweet girl. Want you to strangle it so I know you've gotten yours."

"Just—" Another moan, this one deeper and longer. "A little…faster…"

I pounded harder, circling her little clit in the same rhythm. Working her body with mine until she locked her muscles down. Until her walls clenched so hard around my cock, I was afraid to move, to pull out even an inch for fear of not being able to get back inside. Amazing. Fucking amazing. And completely mine.

When she started to relax, I pumped hard and fast again until I reached my own end. Until I came in long, hot spurts inside of her. Until I filled her up as we both wanted. Until my seed was planted deep inside of her, her womb bathed in my come.

And fuck, did I want to go again immediately at that thought.

"Holy shit, I didn't know it'd be like *that*."

I dropped my head to her chest, lightly biting her breast to get her to yelp. "I think we've got this sex thing pretty well worked out."

"Does that mean no more practicing?"

I rolled us over, grabbing her by the hips to keep us together. Loving how wet our connection was. That it was both of us. "Do you want to stop practicing?"

"Hell no."

"Good, because I've got plans for you."

"What kind of plans?"

I yanked her down by her neck for a kiss before nudging her until she sat up. "I want to watch you ride my cock."

She placed her hands on my chest, a move that

pushed her breasts together and reminded me of my shower fantasy.

"And I still want to titty-fuck you."

"Just those two things and then we'll be done practicing?" Her voice teased, her words said in jest, all while she rotated her hips and made me want to flip her and fuck her senseless again.

"Not even close." I tugged her wrist until she fell onto my chest, until I could rub my nose against hers and hold her to me. "I want to make love to you in the shower. I want to fuck you on the kitchen counter. I want to eat that sweet pussy every single morning before breakfast. I want to finger you while we're in the car and sneak you into the firehouse so I can pump you full of my come in the fire truck." I kissed her lips again, unable not to. Needing her close so she could hear my words. "And I want to put a baby in you. I want to watch you swell with my child. I want to rub your tired legs at the end of a long day and play with your sensitive nipples until I make you come over and over again. I want to be there when this baby is born, and every one after that. Want to be the first man to hold them all. I want everything with you. Every moment, every memory, every fantasy. All of it."

"John." Her voice sighing my name made me want to kiss her all soft and sweet, so I did. A lot. For long stretches of time. Long enough for me to grow hard inside of her once more. For her to start to wiggle over my hips and groan at the contact.

"Ride me," I whispered against her lips. "Ride me

like my cock is the only thing you want. Like *I'm* the only thing you want."

"You are. You're the only one I've wanted for so long."

"Show me, sweet girl." I pushed her up, holding on to her hips as she groaned at how deep I slid inside her. "Get yourself off on my cock while I watch. Make me yours like I made you mine."

She dug her fingers into my chest, making me buck. Making me groan as she whispered, "I've been yours for a long time. You just didn't know it."

Oh fuck. There was no way I was lasting. Not with the view of her on top of me, those hazel eyes I loved so much closed in pleasure. Not with her tits swinging in my face.

Not with all the things I still wanted to do with her playing out in my mind.

"I'm all yours, Em. Whatever you need. Whatever you want. Yours."

And I was. As much as she was mine, I was hers. And I'd do anything to keep her.

chapter eight

EMERY

IT'D BEEN TEN days of pure bliss. Ten days of John loving on me any chance he got. Ten days filled with more orgasms than I'd had the ten *years* prior. And when he'd said he was in this with me, he'd meant it, having spent every night he wasn't working at my place. When he'd been away from me, when he'd had shifts at the firehouse, he'd spent those forty-eight hours texting me whenever he could—the dirtiest, filthiest things, followed by words that made me swoon. Getting me worked up for him, getting me so ready I didn't complain when he walked through the door, those heavy, heated eyes landing on me, and pounced.

It was almost like he was making up for lost time. For all the months we'd wasted by not being together since he'd been back home. And though part of his reasoning for that—our family's reaction—still loomed over us, he'd seemed to have blocked it out. Or rather, he ignored it entirely.

We'd have to tell them eventually—and soon. I didn't want to suddenly show up pregnant with John's baby and give my dad a heart attack. Finding out his baby girl was having a baby of her own was going to be enough of a shock. Pregnant with his stepson's child? Well, that was stroke territory, and I'd rather avoid it entirely. But we had a little time, so I was content following John's lead for now.

I'd been tracking my cycle religiously, using the ovulation sticks every morning. Except today. I'd been late to work—all thanks first to John's tongue, then his cock—so I hadn't had a chance to check. Each day, I'd held my breath, excitement and nerves swirling in my stomach, as I'd waited for the readout. Both terrified and exhilarated to be with John for something more than practice. Of course, the practice was amazing, but to have him inside me, filling me…knowing the possibility of a baby was real? I couldn't wait for that digital readout to tell me the time was right.

After a long day of work, I pulled up to the cottage, glancing down at my phone as it chirped from my purse. Smiling when I saw who the message was from.

It's almost dinnertime and these guys are making spaghetti again. I'd rather have your soft pussy for dinner. Would you like that, sweet girl? If I came home and had you ride my face?

I flushed, going from zero to sixty in half a second flat. My body responding to him as sure as if he were sitting right next to me, whispering the words into my ear as he teased my pussy with his fingers.

Biting my lip, I typed out a response, smiling when I hit send.

I'd love it—I think I proved that this morning when you had me for breakfast...

Smiling the whole way inside, actually, thinking about him reading my text while surrounded by a dozen firefighters. Not able to do anything but sit there, silently, letting my words settle over him. Trying with everything in him not to get hard. Trying and failing, probably.

I tossed my purse on the side table, then kicked off my heels, my sore feet sighing in relief. Today had been exhausting, too many fires to put out, which had meant a late night. It was already nearing seven, and I was wiped. I had nothing on the docket tonight but pizza and mindless TV. But first...I needed to do my daily ovulation check. I'd only ever done this in the morning, as recommended, so I wasn't expecting much. But I didn't want to miss a day, just in case. Once done, I set the stick aside then changed into a pair of leggings and a tank, ready to relax for the evening.

On my way out to the kitchen to get dinner, I swung into the bathroom to peek at the display, sure I'd see a clear circle, same as I had the past ten days. Instead, a smiley face flashed back at me from the digital readout.

"Oh my God," I breathed, my heart rate spiking, elation swirling in my stomach. This could actually be it. I knew the probability of getting pregnant the first month was slim, but it didn't stop the burst of excitement at the possibility.

But, of course, now that I'd finally gotten a smiley face, John had just started a forty-eight-hour shift that morning. Even though he was stuck there for another thirty-six hours or so, I couldn't keep this to myself. And I didn't have anyone else to call—didn't have anyone else who would even care about it. So I pulled out my phone and typed a text to John, snapping a quick pic of the smiley face on the stick and sending it along with two words.

It's time.

He'd stood over me enough in the past few days, waiting for the smiley face, that he'd know what the picture was, would know what it meant. After a few minutes and still no response from him, I set the stick down, washed my hands, and tried to put it out of my mind as I popped a single-serving pizza into the microwave. This was the first day I'd gotten a positive result, which meant we had days to take advantage of it. Even though John had to work two of them, we'd be able to get in some practicing. Well…more than practicing now. It was *time*. But with him at the firehouse for the foreseeable future, I might as well get my mind off that smiley face.

Dinner finished, I was half an episode into a home improvement show when the front door banged open, sending me shooting six inches off the cushion, a scream lodged in my throat. I whipped my head toward the noise, and there he stood. My hulking beast, eyes heated as he stared at me.

"John…what are you doing home?" Except I had a pretty damn good idea, especially when he stalked toward me, gripping the neck of his shirt and whipping it off before tossing it to the side. "You're in the middle of a shift."

"I got coverage. We're going to have a talk about you not locking this door again, but first, it's time to make a baby." He tugged me up from the couch, pulling me against him and descending on me. His mouth hot and hungry against mine, his tongue insistent.

I groaned, melting into him, running my hands over his arms, his shoulders. No longer surprised by what I found, but no less in awe. This big, muscled, perfect specimen of a man was…mine. And he was here to give me exactly what I wanted. A baby.

What he wanted as well. "God, sweet girl. I almost came seeing that stupid smiley face. Do you have any idea how hot it is that you're excited to carry my child?"

"Probably as hot as it makes me knowing you're excited to give me one."

With a groan, he cupped my breast through my tank top, his thumb flicking my nipple as his other hand fumbled with my leggings. Quick, jerky motions attempting to get my pants off. Attempting to get me naked as quickly as possible, so he could slide inside me. So he could fill me. As soon as he'd shoved my pants down far enough, he gripped my ass, pulling me up and against him. Slipping his fingers down until he reached my pussy from behind.

"You *are* down to fuck, aren't you? Already so wet and swollen for me. I bet you're dying to ride me so I can fill you up."

I groaned as he played with me, his movements confident and sure. Like he'd been doing it for years rather than mere days. He almost knew my body better than I knew it myself. Wasn't afraid to push me, to see what could drive me crazy. To try things I'd never even thought of.

No time for that tonight, though. At least, not right away.

He spun me around and pushed me forward until I knelt on the couch, forcing me to grip the back as he jerked my leggings down to my knees. Then he unzipped his pants, pulled out his cock, and settled in behind me. Bringing his body right up against mine, his heat seeping into me.

"Gotta go hard, baby. Need to fill you up to plant my baby inside you. I can't wait another fucking second."

Without fanfare, he drove into me, filling me deep. Always filling me so deep. I moaned, pushing against him and silently begging for more. It was never enough with him. I was always so desperate for more.

He gripped my ponytail in his fist, tugging my head back as he scraped his teeth along my neck. All the while he pumped his cock inside me in an unrelenting rhythm, his hips slapping against my ass, using the hand on my waist to pull me back against him. "Fuck, your pussy's so hot tonight. You're burning me up, sweet girl. Have you been needy all day? Been thinking about me? Were your panties wet under that sinful little skirt you wore to work?"

"*Yes*," I said on a moan, knowing I didn't need to, but letting the word pass through my lips anyway. John knew exactly what it did to me when he woke me up with his tongue.

Already, the tension built inside me, my orgasm fast approaching. My pussy fluttering around his substantial girth, sucking him deeper with each stroke. John rested his chest along my back as he dropped his hand from my hip and reached between my legs, circling my clit in the same rhythm he used to fill me.

"I wanna feel you come, Em. Want your pussy to milk every bit of my seed from me. Want to see you dripping with it when we're done." He brushed his lips against the shell of my ear as he whispered the dirty words, then he lowered his head, teeth sinking into my neck at the same time he pinched my clit and snapped his hips harder against me.

I exploded, pulsing around his driving cock, bursts of colors erupting behind closed eyelids as I white-knuckled the couch cushions. "John, John, John…"

"Fuck, Emery. Take it. Take it all." Even while waves still crashed over my body, he thrust hard, stilling so deep and succumbing to his release, his cock twitching as he spilled inside me. As he filled me with his seed.

I dropped my head to my forearms while John panted against my skin, brushing kisses along my neck and shoulders, sliding the strap of my tank top to the side so he could reach more flesh. God, we hadn't even stopped long enough to get undressed. Something that didn't deter John as he rocked inside me, his cock still half hard and getting harder by the second.

Twisting my head, I looked back at him. "Again?"

He pressed a kiss to my lips, slipping his tongue into my mouth even as he worked his cock inside me. Slower than last time, but just as deep. Just as thorough. "You're not dripping with my come yet, sweet girl. I've got plenty more work to do tonight."

chapter nine

JOHN

I MIGHT HAVE broken my woman. Not intentionally, of course, but her voice sounded hoarse from screaming my name, and she panted in a way that spoke to overexertion. She lay facedown on the bed, her tight ass slightly pink from the way I'd grabbed it during our last round of fucking. Still, I couldn't let her go. Couldn't stop touching her. Couldn't stop trying to please her.

"Oh God, not again." She smacked at my hand, missing completely. I chuckled and kept rubbing from her tailbone to the tops of her thighs. Something about the feel of her skin under my fingers, about the softness of her, drove me absolutely wild in a way I'd never experienced. The ten days leading up to this one had only been an appetizer. Now that I knew it was the right time to get her pregnant? To give us both the baby we so wanted? This was the main course.

And I was ready to gorge myself on her.

"Not done yet." I nipped her shoulder blade, laying one leg across the backs of hers.

Emery turned her head to look me in the eye before huffing a breath that made a lock of her hair fly up. "You got your wish—I'm definitely full of you."

"I can always give you more."

"I don't think I can take more."

Yeah, I'd probably gone a little overboard. "Fine. Then let me rub you. I don't want your muscles to be sore."

"Mhmm…I know how this is going to go. You start with a massage, and pretty soon, I'm halfway to an orgasm."

She didn't lie.

"Are you complaining?"

"You know I'm not."

Figured as much. I rubbed up and down her back, keeping the pressure from my hands steady. Even though I'd been inside this woman a number of times already, even though my legs positively ached from fucking her so long, I wanted her. I wanted to slide between her thighs and thrust deep once more. Wanted to rock in and out until she clenched around me and I once again flooded her womb with my come. I wanted her pregnant so bad, I couldn't think of anything else. Which was why I let my fingers slip down between her cheeks, why I couldn't hold back the needy groan when I felt how wet she was from our mingled release.

"John, I'm sore." Her whiny moan should have

made me stop, but I heard the tinge of need there. The desire that matched mine.

"Tell me no, and I'll stop. You know this." The way she hummed and angled her hips for more certainly seemed like permission, so I slipped a finger inside her, pressing my hardening cock against her hip as I bit down on her shoulder again. "Fuck, it's not enough. I can feel how much I've filled you, and it's still not enough. I can't help it. Knowing we could be making a baby? That in a couple of months, I could see your belly all round and full with my kid?" Another thrust of my hips as I groaned against her. "That's the biggest fucking turn-on of my life."

"With a swollen stomach comes swollen ankles and a swollen ass, too…"

I licked up her neck, drawing a gasp from her. "And I'll still think you're the sexiest woman on the planet. I'll take care of you through it all. I'll rub your feet, make sure you're eating right, help you stand up when you're too big to do it on your own. Hell, I look forward to all of it. Even you sending me out in the middle of the night for whatever weird cravings you have is something I long for."

"You're so good to me." Emery looked back over her shoulder, shooting me a smile that sent my heart racing even as she spread her legs wider. Inviting me inside. "You're going to be such a good partner…such a good daddy."

Daddy. Holy fucking shit, I'd never thought one word could turn me on so much. And if the way she bit her lip was any indication, she knew what she was doing.

"You're killing me, sweet girl." I slipped between her thighs, pinning her down with my weight. The position kept her legs from spreading around me, but I found the heart of her. Found the heaven only my cock would ever know. As she shifted to make room for me, I nudged my way inside on a groan, wedging a hand under her hip so I could play with her clit. She was already so tired, already sore, but I had to. One more time, I needed her. And if the way she reached back to claw at my ass and lifted her hips to give me room to slide deeper was any indication, she needed me, too.

There was no roughness that time, no pulling hair or biting necks. There was simply Emery and me taking pleasure from one another, giving everything we had to reach a climax together. And when she was done, when her pussy clenched around my cock and milked me for every drop, I slid my hand to her belly and palmed her flesh.

"Soon. Maybe not this month, maybe not next month either, but soon. I'll fill you up until we get a baby in this tummy. I promised you that. I'll live up to my word."

Emery shifted to her side, and I slid into place beside her. Holding her to me. I'd never been a snuggler, but with Emery, things were different. Everything was different. This was my forever, my future. She was going to be the mother of my children. That was a more permanent bond than simple marriage. We would always be linked by the babies we made, and I couldn't wait.

———

"I can get up, John."

I flipped the page, double-checking the diagram before adjusting the pillow under Emery's ass. "The book says thirty minutes, and it's only been ten."

Emery huffed, her irritation belied by the soft smile on her face. "You don't think you're being a little ridiculous?"

"No, I'm being proactive. Gravity helps my warriors find your womb, so we're doing the pillow thing for the full thirty minutes."

"You're obsessed."

I lay beside her, rubbing her tummy, my lips finding that spot behind her ear that made her giggle. "Obsessed with you, yes. Obsessed with fucking you, absolutely. Obsessed with making a baby with you, completely. What's so wrong about that?"

She didn't answer, but her sweet kisses and the way she cupped my face with one hand were enough. It'd been two days since she'd sent me the text saying it was time. Two days of fucking her, feeding her, and taking care of her in every way I could think of. I was exhausted, as was Emery, but it was a happy exhaustion. A hopeful one. And as I lay with my hand once again palming her stomach, as I shot another quick prayer up that I was able to give her what she so desperately wanted, I thanked every deity in the heavens for granting me the chance to make this woman mine. I had been an idiot the past year, but I was beyond that. I wanted a life with Emery, wanted my future and hers interwoven. And I'd do anything to get it.

"John, I know you want me to stay here for the full thirty minutes, but I'm *starving*."

I jumped up, grabbing her ankles to keep her in place. "Don't move. I'll get something for you. What do you want?"

Emery's eye-roll was adorable. "Something of the food variety."

"On it." I slipped on a pair of jeans and grabbed a clean shirt from my bag. Fuck everything else—I could shower later. "Pops' Hops should be open for lunch, and I know how much you love that cheesy soup in the bread thing. I'll grab a to-go order. You stay right here and get impregnated."

Emery's laugh followed me out the door. My mission was to acquire food. I could do that. I could do anything if it meant making her smile. When I hopped up into my truck, I caught my reflection in the mirror. Flushed face, tired eyes, but happy. I looked really fucking happy. That was all Emery, for sure. My girl was pure sunshine in a hot little body, and nothing was better than being with her. Nothing at all.

I hauled ass to Pops' Hops and grabbed Em's lunch, making one more stop for her favorite cookies before heading back. It would take a couple of weeks to know if we'd been successful in our quest to make a baby. The idea of waiting, of not knowing, made my stomach turn, and I knew Emery would be as consumed with this as I would be. Just as worried. I'd need to figure out a way to keep us both distracted. Sex would only work for so long. Maybe I could take her away for a couple of days. A little trip to the mainland would definitely make her smile. Or we could take my boat out onto the lake for a weekend. Just us and the water…that might be even better.

I let those thoughts circle as I unlocked her front door and hurried inside. But the sound of her voice, the obviousness of her talking to someone else, caught my attention.

"I'm fine, Dad. Nothing's wrong."

Dad…which meant my stepdad. My stomach plummeted to my shoes, and the fear of losing Em snaked back around me. We hadn't told anyone about us yet, about our plans. Was she telling him now?

"I haven't been feeling well the last couple of days, that's all."

That hurt, but her words also brought a deluge of guilt with the pain. Fuck me, I was an asshole. She had to lie to her father about where she'd been for the two days we'd been holed up in her bed. Emery wasn't the type to lie—she'd never really gotten into trouble even as a teenager, and she was a good girl at heart. This couldn't be easy on her.

"I will. I'll call you tomorrow. Love you."

I leaned against the doorframe of her bedroom, watching as she hung her head. As she clutched the phone as if in prayer. "Everything okay?"

Emery jumped, her wide eyes meeting mine, a

fake smile spreading across her face. But not before I saw the pain there. The worry. "Everything's fine. That was my dad being…my dad."

I nodded, slowly stepping into the room, not knowing what to say to that. "I brought you those cookies you like. For after the soup."

Emery reached for my hand and tugged me close, giving me the sweetest, softest kiss I ever could have asked for. "Thank you. You're an amazing man, you know that?"

But those words made everything worse in my head. Amazing men didn't make their women lie to their family. Our relationship could drive a wedge between her and her dad or her brothers. It could create problems with her boss if the rumors grew too big. I could be destroying many things she loved, but I was too selfish to stop. Not after I'd finally had the courage to take what I needed. Not with the possibility of my baby in her belly.

God help me, but I'd destroy everything on the island to keep her. A fact which only made me feel worse.

"Why don't you go clean up, and I'll get the food set up in the kitchen?"

Another kiss, another spear to my heart. "Always taking care of me…"

But I wasn't, and I dreaded the day she figured that out.

chapter ten

GOD, I ACHED. Ached in places I didn't even know I could ache in. But even waking up to all kinds of uncomfortable twinges, I wouldn't change the past almost two weeks for anything. I'd never thought sex could be like this. I'd fantasized about it, but even my wildest daydreams didn't hold a candle to the reality. Not of being with John, staring into his eyes as he thrust deep inside me. As he filled me with every inch of him over and over until he made me see stars.

My pussy tingled, the subtle throb in my clit distracting, but not enough for me to wake him. I glanced over as he lay on his stomach, sleeping soundly with his arms thrown overhead. The sheet rode low on his hips, showing off his toned back and the dimples at the base of his spine that I'd licked last night. It was the first morning he hadn't woken me with his face between my legs or his cock already sliding inside.

Exhaustion cloaked him, though that was to be expected considering he'd spent the past two days doing nothing but working hard for my pleasure. As if that wasn't amazing enough, he'd also taken it upon himself to make me breakfast in bed while I'd lain dutifully with a pillow beneath my hips. Under strict orders from him not to move an inch. He'd practically waited on me hand and foot, jumping at even the slightest suggestion from me. Hell, last night he'd gone out at ten o'clock to get a box of brownie mix because I'd mentioned a sudden intense craving for them.

I wasn't even pregnant yet, and already he treated me like a queen. *His* queen.

The least I could do was let him sleep while I prepared him breakfast. I slipped out of bed, careful not to jostle the mattress as I slunk away. I pulled on a pair of sleep shorts and plucked one of John's T-shirts off the chair in the corner before sliding it over my head. Since he'd started staying at my place, he'd made sure the kitchen was stocked with more than ice cream and frozen dinners, so I knew I'd have no problem whipping up some eggs and bacon for him.

Fifteen minutes later, the bacon sizzled as the vegetables finished sautéing, ready for the whipped eggs. I poured them into the pan, humming to myself as I thought of what John would say when I brought this in to him. Eyes sleepy, smile quick and free-flowing, he'd pull me into his side, make me curl right up against him—and probably feed me two bites for every one he fed himself. My gentle giant, always taking care of me.

The doorbell rang as I flipped the last piece of bacon. I wiped my hands on the towel and strode to the front door, peering through the peephole. John's mom stood on my quaint front porch, serene smile on her face, looking like everything was perfectly normal. Like I wasn't on the other side of the door in her son's shirt, still sore from when he'd woken me at three in the morning and taken me nice and slow and deep.

Oh God. John's mom was *here*. While her son— the son no one knew was staying with me—was in my bed. *Naked*.

I spun in a circle, hands fluttering at my sides as I tried to figure out what to do. I couldn't very well ignore her—my car was outside. Sweet Lord, so was John's. There was no avoiding this, no hiding the fact that he was in my house. That wasn't necessarily out of the ordinary—my family stopped by all the time. But this early in the morning while I was obviously fresh out of bed? Shit.

While John hadn't specifically come out and said he didn't want to tell everyone, his unvoiced actions spoke as loud—*louder*—than his words. But there wasn't anything I could do about the situation we found ourselves in now.

Smoothing back my bed head, I pasted on a smile and opened the door. "Yvonne! This is a nice surprise. What're you doing here?"

She leaned in for a one-armed hug, juggling a couple pieces of Tupperware in the other. "Morning, honey. Your father begged me to make some oatmeal cookies. I did, of course—can't say no to the man—but I told him I'd be sending half of them away. He'll eat them in one sitting if I don't!"

I laughed, though it felt forced. Felt like my insides were turning to cement. "I may have seen him do that a time or two."

"I'm sure you know all about it." She patted my hand, then stepped inside. "I'll put these in the kitchen for you."

"Um, sure. Thanks for thinking of me." Hands wringing, I followed on her heels, glancing down the hallway toward the open door of my bedroom. Praying John would stay sleeping and I could make something up if I had to. Get her to leave as soon as possible.

"Smells good!" she said.

"Oh, thanks." I hurried over to stir the eggs before turning off the burners and removing the pans from the stove. "Just making some breakfast..." Some breakfast that was obviously too much for only me, the discarded shells of half a dozen eggs stacked in the empty carton I hadn't yet thrown away.

Should I get two plates out? Or should I pretend like I always cooked this much food and then just... didn't eat it? Maybe she'd play along like nothing was unusual. Maybe she'd pretend for everyone's sake.

"Is John here?" Yvonne asked as she took a seat at the dining table. "I saw his car out front."

And there it was. No playing along. No pretending. And definitely no getting around this.

I swallowed, attempting to impart some moisture to my suddenly dry mouth. "Um, yeah. He's—"

"Is that bacon?" John said as he turned the corner into the kitchen, sweat pants hanging indecently low, held up seemingly only by the biteable curve of his ass. He scratched his bare stomach and stifled a yawn before freezing when his eyes landed on Yvonne. "Mom? What are you doing here?"

She lifted a single eyebrow as she gave him a quick once-over. "I could ask you the same thing."

John recovered much quicker than I did, walking straight to the cupboard that held the plates. He pulled a couple down before nudging me over to sit next to Yvonne at the table. "You won't, though."

Yvonne's lips dipped down at the corners as she glanced over at me before bringing her attention back to John. "No, I won't. There are some things even a mother doesn't need to know. Now if your father were still alive—"

"Mom." John's tone brooked no argument. It was one of finality. A warning in a single syllable.

Yvonne rolled her eyes, then turned to me, placing her hand on top of mine as it rested on the table. "Emery, I hope you're feeling better. Your dad said you were sick. It looks like you're able to keep some things down now." She lifted her chin to the food John had slipped in front of me as he settled in a chair with his own plate.

I glanced down at the eggs and bacon I'd made

for John in an effort to be good to him for once instead of the other way around. And suddenly my excuse of being sick didn't seem like merely an excuse, after all. My stomach churned as dread worked its way through my body. I hated lying. More than that, I hated that I needed to. "Um, yeah. Just a little bug, I think. I'm feeling better now."

John dug into his eggs, content to let silence reign, but I couldn't eat. Not even when he nudged my fork toward me, still silent. I hadn't exactly been expecting a declaration at an inopportune time like this, but was he seriously going to sit there and pretend like this was all normal? Like it was perfectly acceptable to be at my house at eight in the morning, wearing only sweat pants, and eating breakfast with me? Apparently.

"Cookies probably won't be good for you yet," Yvonne said, breaking the overpowering silence, "but don't let my son eat everything I brought you. He can be greedy when he wants to be." She shot John a look, her lips pursing to the side as she studied him.

He ignored that, instead asking, "You going out to the cemetery today?"

"Of course," she said. "I go every year. You know that."

I barely had time to register the fact that they were talking about cemeteries and the whys for that when John pushed away from the table, already finished with his breakfast.

"I do." John nodded as he slipped behind me, running a single finger along my shoulders, before leaning down to hug his mom. "I'll talk to you later."

He might as well have said, *Time to get the hell out, Mom.* The directive was clear, though. To everyone.

"You'd better." She sat for a moment, staring up at him once he stood to his full height, her eyes shining in the light. "Be a good man." Her voice cracked, but she cleared her throat no doubt in an attempt to conceal it. She turned her face away and grabbed her bag as she stood to leave.

I stood, too, uncomfortable in my own home. Uncomfortable in my own *skin*, the lies I'd told Yvonne and my dad still bitter on my tongue. The possible repercussions sitting heavy in my gut.

A soft smile curved her lips as she rested her hands on my shoulders then pulled me in for a hug. "Come see your father today. He's worried about you."

I swallowed down the sudden lump in my throat, blinked back the burn in my eyes. I couldn't speak, too fearful I'd open my mouth and cry instead, so I nodded. She pulled back, offered John one last look, then slipped out the front door.

John stood at the sink, rinsing his breakfast plate, before loading it into the dishwasher. Then he grabbed the pans and began washing them, all the while remaining silent. Like this was any other morning. Like this wasn't a big deal. Like his mom hadn't walked in on him here. In an obvious state of undress. With his stepsister. Like I hadn't lied to her, hadn't lied to my dad the other night. Like I wasn't sick about the whole damn thing.

"You're not going to say anything?" I finally asked when the silence got to be too much.

"About what?"

"About *what?* Are you serious?" I slammed my hand on the table, the frustration and anger and… *hurt*…too much to keep bottled up inside. "About the fact that your mom was here and you're there all—" I gestured to his bare back, the defined V of his hips on full display. God, if I looked hard enough, I could see the outline of his cock behind the thin cotton. No. There was definitely no mistaking exactly what had been going on before Yvonne had arrived. "And now you have nothing to say? I lied to your mom, John. I *lied* to her." My voice cracked, the repercussions of what we'd done weighing down on me—not just being together, but keeping it from our family. *Lying* about it.

He braced his hands against the counter, his head hanging as he blew out a sigh. "I'll take care of it."

"What does that mean?"

"It means I'll take care of it." Once done with the dishes, he wiped his hands on the towel before tossing it to the side. He walked over to me, brushing a kiss on my forehead on his way toward the bedroom. "Why don't you eat your breakfast? I need to head into the station for a bit."

I sat in the chair, staring after where he'd gone as sounds of John getting ready filtered down the hallway. The station? I had John's schedule memorized, and I knew for a fact he had today off. He'd found someone to cover his regular forty-eight on shift when I'd gotten the first sign on the ovulation tester, which meant he was just at the start of his standard two days off.

As if it weren't bad enough that we were lying to our family, now he was lying to *me*?

Minutes later, he walked out of the bedroom in jeans and a T-shirt, baseball cap pulled low over his eyes. "Hey." He slipped a finger under my chin, tipping my face up to look at him. "I won't be gone long. And don't stress about my mom. I'll talk to her."

Then he dropped a chaste kiss on my lips and walked away. Leaving me sitting with all these emotions swirling inside me—anxiousness and anger and *hurt*. Uncertainty so deep it was all I could think about. My heart full of pain caused by the one person I never thought would do such a thing.

chapter eleven

JOHN

I ROARED DOWN the coast of the island, trying to clear my head. Fuck, I'd messed up with Em. I knew it—had recognized the stiff set to her shoulders and the anger in her voice—but I couldn't stop myself from letting it happen. All night, I'd been thinking about how she'd had to lie to her dad about me… about us. She shouldn't have had to do that. Not ever. Being with me came with a burden for Emery, something I needed to fix. Something I couldn't shy away from.

I'd wanted to talk to Emery about family stuff over breakfast, plan out what we were going to do and say, but we hadn't been alone as I'd expected to be. Waking up to my mom being in Em's house had thrown me for a loop. It had also made the guilt embed its claws deeper as my girl had been forced to lie to my mother. The two women in my life at odds, and it was my fault.

I was going to make it up to them individually, which was why I'd needed to leave so fast. My mom's presence had reminded me of what day it was and the respect that needed paying.

It'd been more than a decade since I'd made this drive, since I'd stood on a plot of land no one ever wanted to have to buy. I should have gone as soon as I'd gotten home, but…I hadn't. I'd let things get in the way, let my life roll on without thought to my past. But now, I needed to. My mom needed me to. I owed her.

I parked behind her car as she opened the door. The look she shot me was part relief, part irritation, and all mom.

"Did you even bother trying to drive the speed limit, John Michael?"

Ah, the middle name. She liked to pull that out when she was pissed at me. Guess I deserved it. I grabbed her arm when I reached her, grinning as I guided her toward the grass. "Good morning to you too, Mom."

"I already said good morning back at Emery's place." Her steely gaze flicked my way. "I'm going to need an explanation for that one, son."

She'd get no argument from me.

"Yes, ma'am." I walked with her across the grassy rise and past the stones that marked other gravesites, ignoring them all. Those people weren't who we were here to see. Our spot was at the far end of the section, closest to a row of lilac bushes my mother had helped plant. Closest to the lake.

My father's grave.

Mom stopped first, taking a deep breath and clutching my arm a little tighter. She moved to kneel, but I held her up, taking that spot instead. Dropping down to clear off the grass and leaves from the stone with his name carved in it. My name, too.

John Michael Hamilton. Beloved husband and father. The words carried more weight now to me than ever before because of Em. Because of what we were trying to do. Because of what I wanted… with her.

My mom sighed once the stone was clear, sounding tired. Old beyond her years, really. "You didn't have to come, you know."

"I haven't been since before I left for the Corps. I figured it was time."

"I remember that day." She laughed softly, resting a hand on my shoulder. "You were such a young thing then—all skin and bones and gangly limbs. My Bambi in a Marine Corps costume."

"It wasn't a costume."

"No, it wasn't. And neither was your father's, no matter how much he seemed like a boy playing at being an adult when I met him." She dropped down beside me, leaning against my arm. "I still miss him every day."

That took me aback. "But you have Wade now."

"I do, and I love him dearly. He didn't replace your father's hole in my heart, though. Just like I didn't replace the hole left when Wade's wife died. Love doesn't stop or end. Love burrows into our hearts and makes a nest. A permanent one." She bumped me with her elbow. "You should know that. I saw the way you looked at Emery. I've been seeing it since you finally came home."

I jerked back, my brow tight. My shock hardly tempered. "You have?"

"You're my son. Of course I have."

"And that never…bothered you? Since you're married to her father?"

She cocked her head, an almost confused look on her face. "What should that have to do with anything? You two aren't related, and you didn't grow up together. You were long gone when Wade and I got married, and Emery was practically an adult."

But the guilt whispered to me, making me doubt. "I worry about what people will think. What Wade and the boys will think."

"Oh, they'll think you're an asshole for daring to date the precious Emery. They all still see her as a child. Hell, one of the twins might try to fight you, knowing them. They might even be angry enough to win."

I rolled my eyes at her snorted laugh. "Gee. Thanks for sugarcoating that."

She leaned into my shoulder, her body so much smaller than mine. "Emery's not a child, though. Is she?"

"No."

Mom hummed. Nodded. "You love her."

"I do." The answer came quickly. I'd loved her as a friend for years, had lusted after her since I'd moved home, but breaking through that wall and actually spending time together in person? Exploring her body and seeing her kindness and strength? Yeah, I loved her. No doubt.

And my mom apparently already knew it. "Have you told her that?"

"Not yet."

"You should."

"I know. It's all so new, and with the baby thing—"

"What baby thing?" Her eyes went wide, something close to fury swirling through them. "John Michael Hamilton Junior, I swear to God, if you weren't careful with her after all the times I showed you how to put on a condom—"

"Ma, stop." Those were definitely memories I didn't need to relive. The joys of being raised by a single mom—I hadn't eaten a banana in years because of those lessons. "I didn't get her pregnant on accident. She…wants a baby. With me. Before…"

I couldn't say the words, but my mom knew. Of course she did. The Collins' family history was well-known.

"Oh," she breathed, sitting back down on her calves. "Before having her ovaries removed so she doesn't get sick like her mom did."

"Yeah."

Mom sat silent for a long moment before quietly asking, "And do you want—"

"More than anything."

"You didn't let me finish."

"You don't need to." I turned to fully face her, holding her gaze as I unburdened my truth. "I want her. I have since I moved home and realized my best friend—the woman I'd been sharing my secrets with for years through letters and emails—wasn't a little kid anymore. And I want a baby, I want a family. I want all that with her. Want it so bad, it hurts."

The smile pulling at her lips tempered her sigh. "You're going to have to tell Wade and the boys."

"I'm planning to."

"Soon?"

I looked over the stone in front of me again, the one with my name on it. Focusing on the dates this time. "Today."

She chuckled, pushing on my shoulder as she rose to her feet. "On your father's birthday. Fitting. I remember him standing in front of my own father and brothers—in his uniform, no less—asking for their blessing to marry me."

I ran my finger over the name etched in marble one last time before getting to my feet. "Do you ever wonder what would have happened if they wouldn't have given it?"

"Oh, honey. He asked for their blessing, not their permission." She grabbed my arm again as we headed for our cars. "Your father and I were in love—nothing could have stopped us from being together."

Nothing. She said the word like she meant it, with a fire and a sureness that brooked no argument.

I understood that because I felt the same way about Emery. Nothing would get in our way.

When we reached the road, I opened her car door and helped her inside. My pulse raced with my need to get back to Em, but I had one more thing I needed to say to my mom.

Before she could shut the door, I leaned down to kiss her cheek. "Thanks, Mom."

A confused sort of smile graced her pretty face when I pulled away. "For what?"

"For being you."

She waved me off, but I could see the redness around her eyes. Could see how much the words meant to her. My mom may have been made of steel, but she was a softy when it came to her only child.

Once her door was closed, she rolled down her window and started the engine, leaning out and grabbing my wrist one last time. "You are your father's son, John. Always have been. Just as stubborn and determined, just as brave."

"He was a good man."

"As are you." She let me go and put the car in gear. "Now, go home to your girl, John Michael. I have a feeling you have some apologizing to do."

Fuck, she wasn't wrong. I hurried to my truck, the engine rumbling as I turned the ignition. It was time to go home and deal with the shit I'd been ignoring for weeks. Time to be the man my father would have wanted me to be.

I followed my mom down the coast until she turned off toward her house, then I sped off for the cottage. All the way, the final words she'd said swirled in my head. Apologize? I needed to beg Em for her forgiveness. I needed to tell her how much I loved her. We'd deal with her family together, but no matter what, I wanted to be with her. And I needed to make sure she knew that.

But when I walked into the house, instead of anger or yelling, silence greeted me. Well, not completely.

"Hey, baby." I stared at Em's back, waiting for a response. One I didn't receive. She cleaned instead—scrubbed, really. Hunched over the kitchen floor on her hands and knees, scouring the tile with a sponge. The only answer I received was a look shot over her shoulder. I didn't need more to know what was going on—her eyes were red-rimmed, her face flushed but streaky. Emery had been crying, and that was one hundred percent my fault.

Fuck.

I set my keys on the counter, the one that looked as if she'd already cleaned it within an inch of its life. I had no idea Formica could actually…sparkle. "Em? What are you doing?"

"Cleaning the floor." The eye-roll was implied, though I wouldn't have been surprised to see it.

This would not end well.

"Why don't you let me help you?"

She jerked back onto her heels and tossed the sponge into the bucket next to her. Water splashed up over the sides, marring the clean floor. Something she didn't even seem to notice. "How was the station?"

Time to man up. "I didn't go to the station."

"Yeah, no shit." She jumped to her feet, grabbing the bucket and stalking to the sink. I assumed she'd dump the dirty water there. But instead, she grabbed a different sponge and began a full-on assault on the stainless-steel vessel. Back straight. Shoulders stiff. Angry.

"Em, listen—"

"You lied to me." Her words landed like daggers, wounding me as they struck.

"I did, and I shouldn't have resorted to that. My mom being here this morning threw me for a loop."

"You don't think it threw me for a loop? You don't think it affected me at all?"

"I'm sure it did, which is part of why I went after her. I knew she was heading to the graveyard, and I needed to have a conversation with her. About us. I needed her to understand."

She huffed again, shaking her head. "And you didn't think I should be a part of that? Didn't think I should be involved—even in the barest sense of you telling me what you were doing—at all?"

"In hindsight, yeah. Of course. At the time…I wasn't thinking straight." Which was an understatement. Not that she needed to hear that.

Emery tossed the sponge down, her face hard when she finally turned my way. Guard up. "It felt like you weren't thinking at all—and certainly not about me. What we're doing…our future with a baby… It's supposed to be a partnership, John. I don't want any of this to be one-sided, and that's exactly what you made it."

"Emery, I'm—"

But she didn't let me finish. Instead, she threw her hands in the air and stormed off down the hallway, slamming the bedroom door when she disappeared inside. Leaving me alone.

I ran a hand over my face, scratching the scruff on my chin. I needed to find a way to get Emery to listen to me so I could apologize to her. So I could explain. I certainly hadn't done a good job of that so far, but I'd keep trying. I had to.

Resigned to being yelled at again, I slipped down the hall to the bedroom door. I hated that it was closed, that she was hiding from me. I wanted to break the fucker down, but I knew better. Still, keeping my brain in control of my body took more effort than I cared to admit.

"Baby? Em?" I knocked once, glaring at the slab of wood between us. "I know I screwed up, but please come out and talk to me."

Silence.

I knocked again, practically shouting. "Emery."

The door whipped open, and one sour-faced woman flew past me. She never even glanced my way. "I wanted to have a discussion this morning, but you were silent. Now, I'm not much in the mood to talk."

My blood froze as she grabbed her keys and purse. "You can't leave."

Wrong thing to say.

Emery spun, eyes narrowed, lips curled into what I could only describe as a snarl. "Watch me."

The front door slamming behind her might as

well have been a gunshot for the hole it ripped in my chest. Emery had left me. Gone. She ran away, putting physical space between us. I could handle her being mad; I could understand it and accept it. But leaving?

I paced the living room, considering my options. There was really only one, though. That woman was my life and could very well be carrying my child. She wanted space? Too fucking bad. I may have screwed up this morning, but I knew we could fix that. I'd beg, borrow, or steal to make her believe my apology if I had to.

But first, I needed to find her.

chapter twelve

EMERY

STORMING INTO MY childhood home after a fight with a boy was something altogether new for me. Hell, being with a man at all was something I had absolutely zero experience with. Something my dad made perfectly clear when I flew through the front door, cheeks flushed, eyes red-rimmed and glassy, and he looked at me as if I were a ghost.

"Emmy?" he asked, eyebrows shooting toward his hairline. "What's going on? Is everything all right?" He did a quick scan of me from head to toe, flitting his eyes briefly near my stomach, panic written all over his face.

Wade Collins was the most fearless man I'd ever known…except when it came to his only daughter. Though he hadn't expressed it in so many words, his worry for me had always been plain as day. Worry that I'd follow in my mom's footsteps. That a ravaging disease would take me too soon. A fear that only worsened around the anniversary of her death, which was next month.

"It's not anything like that, Daddy." I gave him a hug, intent on reassuring him. Instead, my eyes burned as I settled into arms that reminded me of a happy childhood despite everything we'd gone through and tried my hardest not to cry.

"Wade?" Yvonne called from another room. "Is that Emery?"

"Yeah, honey. She's, uh…" He thumped his hand on my back. "Maybe you could come out here?"

While my dad had never shied away from showing his affection with hugs, he'd also never had to deal with his daughter blubbering all over him. I'd never had a reason to.

"Emery, I'm so glad you… What is it?" Yvonne asked, stepping into the room.

"It's nothing. I'm fine." I pushed away from my dad, discreetly wiping my eyes as I slipped over to the couch and sat down, pretending like everything was okay. Like the man I'd asked to give me a baby hadn't just stomped all over my heart with his careless disregard for my concerns and feelings.

But Yvonne had been a mom for a long time, and my dad was the chief of police—it was their jobs to spot bullshit. There was no way I was getting anything past them.

She shot my dad a look—one I pretended not to see—then tilted her head in my direction, eyebrows raised. "You two should talk. I'll go make some coffee."

My dad stared after Yvonne's retreating form, looking as lost as I'd ever seen him. He cleared his throat, then crept toward the couch to settle on the cushion next to me. "Do you…do you want to talk about it?"

Even though I was upset, I couldn't help but laugh at how uncomfortable he was. I shook my head. "Not yet. I just wanted to be home. And Yvonne said you were worried about me."

"Yeah. Wanted to make sure that bug was gone. You feeling better?"

And just like that, everything came flooding back. I hated having to lie to him, hated every second of it. I wanted to tell them everything, wanted to share with both of them—my brothers, too—the fact that I was involved with an amazing man who made me happy…most of the time. A man I was in love with. A man I wanted to have a baby with. A man who just happened to be my stepbrother.

I opened my mouth to say something—what, I had no idea—when the front door burst open, and John flew inside, eyes wild as he scanned the room. "Emery." As soon as he spotted me, he heaved a sigh, his entire body relaxing. "I hoped you'd be here."

My shoulders stiffened, my spine straightening. I had absolutely no desire to air our dirty laundry at our *parents'* house. "I thought it'd be obvious by the way I left that I wanted some time away from you."

John shook his head and took a step toward

me. "Not like this. Not when you're mad. Let me make things right again, then you can go do things without me." Brows drawn down, he frowned. "For a little while."

Before I could respond, Yvonne came around the corner carrying a carafe and mugs. She shot her son a smile. "I figured you'd show up here. Want some coffee?"

"Wait…what do you mean you figured he'd show up here? What's going on?" Dad asked, glancing first at Yvonne, then to me, before finally settling on John. John, whom I refused to look at, too scared that if I did, I'd melt into a puddle right here on the couch. I was still mad, still *hurt*, and I wanted to hold on to that a bit longer.

"Nothing," I said, attempting to end the discussion.

John had other ideas. "Your daughter and I had a disagreement this morning. Completely my fault, sir."

"Is that so?" My dad assessed John differently now, his confusion turning into suspicion in two seconds flat. "A disagreement about what?"

As hard as I tried to keep my attention off John, my eyes were drawn to him. To his huge presence in this small room. He glanced at me, meeting my gaze briefly, before straightening to his full height, perfect posture in place as he addressed my father. "I didn't communicate well with her, sir, and ended up hurting her feelings. Something I deeply regret."

"I see," my dad said, the words clipped, his eyes narrowed as he studied John.

"Why don't we give these two a second alone, Wade?" Yvonne pulled my dad to his feet. "Let them work things out."

"But—"

"Come on, now. I saved some of those cookies for you." She linked her arm through my dad's and guided him into the kitchen even as he dragged his feet, shooting glances over his shoulder toward us.

At least their being in the other room gave us the illusion of privacy. Trouble was, I didn't know if I wanted to be alone with John right then. I was still too emotional over everything, and I knew if I looked at him, if I listened to him, I'd forgive, just like that.

John crouched in front of me, resting his elbows on bent knees and bringing us to eye level. "I was an idiot this morning."

I raised an eyebrow. Stating the obvious wasn't going to win him any points with me. "Yes, you were."

He reached out, pulling one of my arms away from my chest, then encased my hand between both of his. "I'm sorry, baby. I need you to know that, first and foremost. I never meant to hurt you."

"Well, you did." I tried to yank my hand away, but he held tighter, his fingertips tracing over my skin in a soft caress. As good as it felt, especially after the morning, I couldn't lose sight of the issues we needed to discuss. "You ignored my concerns when I brought them up. You brushed them aside as if they didn't matter, which made me feel like *I* didn't matter. You acted as if you could snap your fingers and take care of everything. Things don't work like that, John. Not with me."

"You're right—I did all of that. It's not what I intended, though. I would never—*ever*—purposely make you feel as if you didn't matter. You matter so much, I can't think straight at times. I wanted to take care of you this morning, to protect you from anything negative. I handled it wrong—I see that now. But it wasn't because you didn't matter. The opposite, really. Your happiness is everything to me, and I didn't want you to be stressed about stuff I thought I should deal with."

Rolling my eyes, I huffed. "But not talking about things doesn't magically make them go away. And then for you to flee before discussing things with me, to leave me out completely as if this doesn't affect me? That was a shitty move. And to top it all off, you *lied* to me."

"I did. I fucked up. I should've told you I needed to be with my mom, but I was focused on the mission. That's not an excuse, though. I know it." He slid his hands up my thighs, bunching my maxi skirt as he went. Then he gripped my hips, his fingers digging into my ass as he tugged me forward. "I don't make the same mistakes twice."

The very thing I'd worried would happen was happening. I was melting. Right here, on my dad's couch, with John nestled between my spread legs, his hands massaging my hips and ass. Thank God I'd worn a long skirt. It gave at least the illusion of a barrier, flimsy as it was—especially if John made it his mission to get under it. Even with the sexual tension brewing between us, I needed to make sure what went on this morning wouldn't happen again.

"You better not." I rested my hands on his biceps, forcing myself to keep my fingers still. Not to caress the bulk of muscles there, not to slide my hands under the sleeves of his T-shirt to feel his skin against mine. "Because if this thing is going to work, you have to be my *partner*."

He scowled, his voice low and grumbly as he said, "There's no if. We'll make this thing work."

"Then there's no more lying. Period. I hate it. I hate being the one doing the lying, and I really hate being the one lied to."

"No more lying. Got it." He pulled me even closer so he could brush featherlight kisses along my jaw, nuzzle my neck.

My stomach flipped at the contact, at the way he murmured my name as his lips caressed my skin. "That means we need to tell our family."

"Yeah." He sighed, placing one last kiss behind my ear and pulled back. "I'm here to do that for sure, but I sort of already told my mom."

I jerked my head back, mouth agape as I dug my fingernails into his arms. "You did? Today?" Groaning, I dropped my chin to my chest, before looking up at him. "Oh my God, John, don't tell me I lied straight to her face when she already knew about us!"

"No, no. I told her at the cemetery after she left the house. That's where I went." He linked his fingers together at the small of my back, guiding me even closer to the edge of the couch. Closer to him. "It's my dad's birthday today. I knew she'd go there, and I haven't been to pay my respects since I've been back."

The small bit of fight remaining inside me fizzled out completely. I knew what it was like to visit a parent's gravesite—knew all about how the supposed-to's and the have-to's didn't always align with the want-to's. I cupped his face, ran my palm over the scruff he hadn't bothered to shave the past few days. "I wish you would've told me. I would've liked to go with you."

"I didn't even remember until I saw her. We can go, though. Maybe drop by your mom's to make sure the stone's cleaned off and in good repair."

God, this man. So sweet. So kind. He'd messed up, without question. But everyone did at some point. The real test was how they made amends for it—if they kept their promise not to do it again. John had promised he wouldn't, and he was a man of his word. I believed him with all my heart.

"Okay." I leaned forward, pressing a soft kiss to his lips. "I'd like that."

"Everything all right in here?" Yvonne called before peeking around the corner from the kitchen. "You two aren't doing anything we wouldn't want to see, are you?"

"Jesus, Mom." John groaned and shook his head. He focused on me, then leaned close and whispered, "Ready for this?"

I took a deep breath, pulling back to look over John's shoulder toward where Yvonne stood, my dad behind her, his brows drawn and mouth cemented in a scowl as he stared at John and me. "Ready."

John pushed to his feet, pulling me up to stand next to him, then turned to face our parents. "Mr. Collins, sir. Emery and I have something we'd like to talk to you about."

"Oh, now it's Mr. Collins, is it?" my dad grumbled, his voice dialed straight to *petulant child*. Or, more aptly, *pissed-off dad*.

"Formal feels more respectful in this situation, sir."

My dad narrowed his eyes even further, straightening to his full height and going into Cop Mode. "I'm listening."

"We're in a relationship, sir. I know that will bring some unwanted attention on the family considering your marriage to my mom, but I refuse to keep Emery at arm's length because of some gossip. I care deeply for her, and somehow I was lucky enough that she feels the same for me. Stepsiblings or not, we're together, sir. Permanently."

My dad glanced between us, and the shock I'd expected to see on his face wasn't there. Instead, he looked as if he'd almost been expecting this. Though, with my dad spending the past thirty-five years of his life as a cop, that wasn't so hard to believe.

"What happens within our family isn't anyone's business but ours." My dad split a look between John and me. And if I hadn't been standing next to him, his arm banded around my back, I wasn't sure I'd have been able to tell how John's whole being seemed to relax at my dad's words.

"Though I'm not sure how this is permanent yet," Dad said. "I don't see a ring."

"Wade," Yvonne admonished, shooting him a glare.

I rolled my eyes, but John didn't back down. Instead, he said, "I haven't asked her to marry me yet, but we're committed to each other nonetheless." He looked down at me as he tucked me closer into his side. "I'd marry her today if she wanted that."

I gasped, shooting my eyes to his as I rested my hand on his stomach. "You would?"

"Now, hold on a minute—" My dad's irate tone drew my gaze for a moment, but even Yvonne's slap to his chest and reprimand for him to hush couldn't keep my attention for long. Not when John slipped a finger under my chin and turned my face back to him.

"Without question," he said, his focus never straying from me. Never once glancing at the pissed-off chief of police a few feet away.

I melted into him, pushing aside the fact that we were standing in front of our parents. "Well, I hope that's not your proposal because it sort of sucked." I bit my lip, attempting to stifle the smile that refused to be confined.

John brought his thumb to my lip, tugging it from my teeth. He traced my upturned mouth, his own mirroring mine. "I'll work on it for next time."

"Let me get this straight," my dad persisted, arms crossed, brows drawn down, even with Yvonne scowling at his side. "You're in a permanent relationship, without a ring, but you're planning on asking her to marry you someday. Have I got that about right?"

I rolled my eyes and shot my dad a look. "You don't have to sound so mad about it, Dad. John's an amazing man—you've said that yourself!"

He scoffed. "Well, I meant in *general.* Not in relation to my baby girl!"

"You're being ridiculous."

"I disagree. But even if you're correct, that's my right as a dad. Need to make sure the man you choose treats you right." Dad glared at John. "And my daughter coming in here with red eyes like she'd been crying doesn't prove that very well."

"Dad—"

"He's right, Em." John leaned down to press a kiss to the top of my head before straightening once again to his full height and addressing my father. "You're right, sir. I've already apologized to Emery, but I'd like to apologize to you as well. I never meant to hurt her. I was an idiot this morning, but it won't happen again. You have my word."

"Awful early in the day to have already screwed up, son." My dad assessed John, shrewd cop cranked up to ten. "What were you doing with Emmy so early?"

Yvonne slapped a hand to my dad's chest. "Oh, Wade. Stop. The kids are too old for us to be worrying about what they're doing every minute of the day."

"She's my baby girl," he said to her, then lifted his eyes to me. "I'll never stop worrying about her."

Part of me softened at the fact that I had such

an amazing man for a father—someone who only wanted what was best for me. But only *part* of me. The other part had to clear something up. "Dad, I can worry about myself."

Apparently, the fact that I shouldn't have to do so was the one thing John and my dad agreed on, if the look they shot each other was any indication.

"I worry enough for both of us, sir," John promised.

"Now you're *both* being ridiculous."

"Oh, honey, this is what they do." Yvonne shook her head, glancing between them. "Sometimes you just need to let them."

Slipping away from my dad, she hurried over to John and me, then guided us straight to the front door. "I'm sure you both would like to be alone for a bit— finish talking and get everything settled. How about dinner tomorrow night? We can chat about things more."

"Thanks, Mom." John broke away from me only to press a kiss to her cheek. "Call if you decide to go back to the cemetery later."

She smiled as she nearly shoved us out the front door. "I have a feeling you'll be busy, but I think I'm okay with that."

"You have any problems at all, you call me, Emmy!" my dad hollered.

Yvonne huffed, then whispered to us, "Don't you worry about him. I'll handle it."

John shot his mom a grateful smile and took my hand as he led us toward the porch steps. "Let's get home, sweet girl."

"Home?" my dad called, his voice sharp. "What the hell does he mean home—"

The front door slammed on my dad's question, and, not for the first time today, I was thankful Yvonne was there to defuse the situation.

Finally just the two of us, I leaned into John's side as he guided us down the front walk to the driveway. "I missed you this morning. I know that's weird because you were there, but it felt off. Wrong. You were distant like you were…before."

"Never again." He opened the passenger's side door to his truck, not pausing as he gripped my hips and lifted me straight up into the seat. "You're mine now, sweet girl. I may not always do the right thing or say the words you need to hear, but I'll always try. I'll always strive to keep us together. I could never go back to the hell that was denying my attraction to you." He pulled out my seat belt and reached around me to lock it into place. "Stay there. We need to get on the road."

"What about my car?"

"We'll come back for it." He gave me a quick kiss before shutting my door and jogging around to his side. Once inside, he put the truck in gear and drove off, taking us in the direction of the cottage. "I don't want you to leave my side right now. Besides, I didn't get to give you a wake-up call this morning. We should remedy that right away."

I laughed, biting my lip as I recalled his favorite way to wake me up. My favorite, too. "Definitely as soon as we get home."

"I've got a better idea." He turned down an uninhabited backroad, not stopping until we parked right by the lake in a thicket of trees. Then he shot me a look as he shut off the ignition. One that could only be read as pure hunger.

I glanced around, seeing everything I needed to in his eyes. "*Here?*"

"Here." He unbuckled my seat belt, then grabbed me by the hips and hefted me across the seat. Not stopping until I sat astride his lap and he had my skirt rucked up around my hips, his already hard cock pressing against me. "We fought today, baby. We need to make up, and I don't want to wait another second."

So he didn't. He captured my lips, releasing a groan into my mouth as soon as his tongue brushed against mine. All the while, his hands were greedy, gripping me wherever he could. Delving into the back of my underwear so he could cup my ass and rock me against him. Not stopping as he slipped his hand between my legs from behind. I read everything I needed to in those actions—he was as desperate for me as I was for him. Our fight may have only lasted a few hours, but it'd felt like a lifetime. It was time to make amends.

"John," I breathed, tilting my head to the side as he scraped his teeth along my neck.

"Gonna make you scream, sweet girl. Out here, in the woods, where anyone could see if they happened past. We'll put on a show, won't we?" He blew a warm puff of air over my nipple even through my shirt before grazing his teeth against it. "Want you so bad, baby. Want to suck all over your tits. Give 'em to me."

Without hesitation, I did as he asked, pulling my shirt up and off. John didn't even wait for me to take off my bra, just dove in with a growl and sucked me straight through the lace. I cried out, gripping the top of the seat behind him as I arched my back, trying to get closer. Always trying to get closer.

John continued to rub my pussy from behind, slicking me up for him. Prepping me to take him inside. And I couldn't wait another minute. I fumbled with the fastenings of his jeans, then wrapped my fingers around his length, stroking from root to tip. So thick. So big. This was still new enough that I marveled at his size every time I touched him. Marveled at how hard and solid he was beneath silky-smooth skin.

"Jesus, I need to be inside you." John slouched down and brought his ass toward the edge of the seat to give me more room, holding my panties out of the way so I could take him inside.

And I did. I gripped his cock and rose up on my knees, then slid down on his thick length, swallowing him whole. Groaning as he filled me. As he stretched me so much, he stole my breath. "Oh my *God*."

"That's my girl. Take it all. You're so nice and wet for me, so hot and soft. Fucking perfect."

I clutched the back of the seat with both hands and lifted up before sinking down, swiveling my hips on each downstroke. He slid so deep like this, made me feel so full, but I loved it. Loved that it seemed like I had all the power here as I rocked over him. As I took him inside again and again, shooting us both straight toward our releases. Seemed like I'd reduced this huge, overpowering man to a pile of helpless need.

"I love it when you ride my cock. Drives me crazy to have you run the show." John gripped my hips, his fingers digging into my ass, careful not to take control of this. I could feel how much he wanted to in every inch of his body. In the stiff set of his shoulders, the sharp tendons of his neck, the bunched muscles of his biceps. So much restrained power, all so I could ride him exactly how I wanted.

But the best part of being with him was how we worked together, and I wanted that now.

"Move with me, John."

He groaned, his hips snapping up as soon as the words left my mouth. "Gonna fuck you so good, sweet girl. Fuck a baby right into you."

Our lips met in a messy kiss, all teeth and tongues, groans from both of us mixing in the middle. When he slipped his thumb between us and traced tight circles around my clit, all the while thrusting into me from below, I couldn't hold back anymore. My eyes fluttered closed as the waves crashed over me while John continued to fill me over and over again until he pushed deep. Settled so far inside me, a groan rumbling from his throat before he breathed my name like a prayer as he came.

I collapsed against his chest, a boneless heap of ecstasy as I tried to catch my breath. "We should fight more if this is what make-up sex is all about."

"I'm all in for more make-up sex. Maybe I can forget to put the toilet seat down or something—you can scold me for it, and then I can bend you over the vanity for the making-up part. That'll count. That'll be enough of a fight."

I laughed against his chest before pushing back to look at him. "I don't know…falling into the toilet in the middle of the night isn't fun."

"But make-up sex *is*."

"You're not wrong."

He reached up and slipped his fingers around my nape, pulling me close. So close his lips brushed against mine as he said, "I never want to have a real fight again, though. Not with you."

"No real fights." I nipped his bottom lip, brushing my hands over his chest and rocking in his lap as he grew hard once again inside me. As he dug his fingers into my hips, pulling and pushing me. Guiding me. "Just amazing sex."

"Amazing sex that leads to babies." He pulled me down on him, filling me completely as he rotated my hips in a circle. Grinding my clit right against him and making me moan. "I'm going to come inside you every day until we make a baby, and then I'm going to come inside you every day because I can. You're my home, Emery. My world. And I can't wait to make a new life with you. I can't wait to have a tiny little you running around and stealing my heart just like her mama did."

My eyes fluttered closed, my heart bursting at his words. "John," I breathed.

"Love you, sweet girl. I have for so long, and I always will. You're mine, and I promise to be good to you."

I never thought I'd hear those words from him. Never thought I'd be lucky enough to call this man mine. Never thought I'd be given the opportunity to make a family with him. To make a *life* with him.

"I love you, John." I whispered the words against his lips, loving how his eyes flared as I said them, how his cock twitched inside me. How he gripped me tighter, held me closer. Whispered my name over and over as he filled me.

Making me feel so safe and cherished and undeniably loved. Making me feel like I was *his*.

epilogue

JOHN

THE PARKING LOT at the old mall was more crowded than it'd been in years as reporters and local businesspeople hurried toward the stage. I hung back, my eyes on my girl. My soon-to-be wife. And the person currently looking like the happiest woman in the world.

Pregnancy agreed with Emery.

But she was busy working for that jackass, Huntley, so I couldn't talk to her. Couldn't pull her close and rub my hand over her belly like I wanted to. At least I was able to be at the event with her. She'd been so busy lately. As soon as the town council had approved the mall rehab project, her schedule had blown up. Even with my two full days off from the station every forty-eight, I wasn't able to spend a lot of time with her because of work. I was itching to get my hands on her.

As I sidled closer to my Em, sticking to the edges of the crowd, I caught sight of someone I knew. Three someones, really. Emery's brothers stood to one side, obviously unhappy. All staring right at me with their arms crossed and their glares firmly in place. Fuck, they simply refused to be adults about everything. Even Jackson, who still hired me for construction projects, couldn't look at me without wearing some sort of a puss. Telling them about Em and me had gone about as well as I'd expected—stitches and all— but I'd assumed we'd have moved past the anger phase already. Apparently, that wasn't happening.

Hopefully, they'd get over their bullshit before the baby was born. That was one bombshell we hadn't dropped on them just yet. No sense giving them another reason to want to kick my ass. Not that they could, at least not without me letting them get in a few shots for good measure.

I mean, I was fucking their baby sister. I deserved a punch or two.

Turning away from the wall of Collinses, I headed back across the lot, spotting a much better person to talk to. My friend and coworker, Riley, stood head and shoulders above most of the crowd, making him easy to spot. I turned his way, arriving in time to hear him talking to the mayor of Temperance Falls—Kate, also known as his brand-new wife.

Their quickie wedding had thundered through the gossip mill on the island long enough that Emery and I were allowed a slow, uneventful shift from adult stepsiblings to romantic couple. I owed him even if he didn't realize it. I would have approached to say thanks, but he was busy arguing with his wife.

"Thirty minutes and we're going home so you can rest."

I could almost hear Kate's eye-roll. I might have said a few things like that to Emery in the past few weeks. Ever since we'd found out she was pregnant, I'd been a bit overbearing.

Fine, I'd been a protective asshole. She carried precious cargo with her—I had a right.

"You're being ridiculous," Kate said. Which was exactly how my sweet girl responded every time I went all careful-daddy on her. I tried not to listen to the conversation, but Riley wasn't exactly quiet and I was about as curious as everyone else on the island.

"Fine. But I'm getting you some fucking crackers and a water."

I glanced up at Emery, frowning. Maybe I should find *her* crackers and water. She didn't suffer from morning sickness like some of the books I'd read on pregnancy had told me to expect, but she was hungrier than usual. For food and for me, thankfully. I was one hundred percent on board with making sure she got what she needed in both respects, but I hadn't paid attention to her breakfast that morning. How could I when I'd been under the table with my face buried between her legs? When she'd grabbed my hair and pulled ged me against her pussy until she'd come twice? Perhaps I'd been too wrapped up in her larger breasts and more swollen, sensitive body to be a good partner to her. To take care of my unborn child. Maybe she was feeling sick, and I simply hadn't noticed.

I'd fucking notice now, though.

I kept my eyes locked on my girl, watching every movement, searching for a sign she needed something. But Emery didn't seem to be bothered by anything. She stood on the stage, a smile on her pretty face as she chatted with her boss. Practically glowing or some shit. She mesmerized me. I was the luckiest motherfucker ever to walk the earth with that woman by my side. I wanted to take her home and prove it to her over and over again, but she had work to do. This ribbon-cutting ceremony shouldn't take too long, though—an hour at most, she'd told me. Then we could head back to our little cottage on the lake where I could strip her out of that pencil skirt she wore and worship every inch of her.

After I made sure she had a good lunch.

When Kate finally headed for the stage, I slipped in next to Riley, still watching Emery for signs she needed me. Still planning all the things I'd do to her once I got her home. "Everything okay over here?"

Riley's shoulders stayed stiff, but his voice held no irritation. Protective mode, and I was definitely not a threat. "What are you doing here, man?"

I spared him a glance, then went back to watching Emery, shrugging in response. "Same thing you are, I suppose."

Kate beelined to Emery's side on the stage, the two leaning closer and chatting while the town council stood off to the side. The two women were a juxtaposition of femininity—Kate all blond and fair, her business suit tailored and crisp, while Emery was darker in hair color with a more golden skin tone. She wore a tight skirt with a loose blouse over it, looking soft and huggable. Fuckable, for sure. Especially since she was carrying my baby.

There was nothing hotter than knowing that.

Riley interrupted my thoughts, leaning closer to whisper, "You and Emery?"

Yeah, apparently that news hadn't made it all the way around the gossip mill yet. Too bad for him. "Don't know what you're talking about." It was at that moment my Emery frowned, looking slightly paler than before. Motherfucker, she *did* need crackers and water. I slapped Riley on the shoulder, too focused on my woman to deal with him anymore. "See you at work."

"Sure will. We can have a chat."

"Fuck your chat." I hightailed it to my truck, berating myself the entire way. I should have been better prepared, should have paid attention to what she'd eaten this morning. Or had she eaten? I'd made her breakfast, but somehow we'd ended up distracted. A great moment for sure, but I'd never actually seen her take more than a bite or two. My bad, and a mistake I wouldn't make again.

I grabbed Emery's bag from the floorboard of the truck and rifled through it, knowing she kept protein bars and various snacks in it.

"Jackpot." I snagged a bottle of water and a bag of cheese-flavored crackers from the depths and tucked the purse back under the seat. The ceremony was starting, but I didn't care. Emery might be sick—everyone else could wait.

Over the speakers, Kate's voice rang out. "Friends and neighbors, we're here to kick off a construction project three years in the making."

I rushed to the back side of the stage, catching Emery's attention as I slipped into a space behind her chair. The stage was high enough for me to hide behind. Mostly. People could probably see my head and shoulders, but I didn't care. My girl needed me.

Girls, really. Genetic tests had already told us what we were having. A mini-Emery would be joining us in January, something I couldn't wait for. She'd be a queen like her mommy—beautiful and smart—but with me teaching her how to be a little badass? The girl was going to rock this island from her first step. I'd already bought her a little onesie that said "Forget the Knight… I Want a Sword" to make it clear she would be no damsel in distress. Pampered? Yes. My princess? Absofuckinglutely. Helpless? Not on my watch.

Six months to go.

"What are you doing back there?" Em's whisper carried no anger, mostly curiosity. And maybe a little mocking. I could take that.

"You looked pale. I brought you water and crackers."

Emery turned enough to catch my eye, a smile on her face that made my heart melt. "I'm fine, but thank you. I got a little queasy. It passed."

"Take them." I pushed the bottle and bag across the stage floor until they rested against her foot. "I don't want you to feel sick."

"Everything okay over here?" Huntley glanced my way, frowning.

"Everything's fine, Mr. Huntley. My fiancé was just—"

"Leaving." I ran a finger along the top of Emery's foot, unable not to touch. "I'll be at the bottom of the stairs when you're through."

Huntley didn't look too happy, but he could take a flying leap. My girls needed me. There was nothing that would ever stand in my way of taking care of them. Not him, not some job, not the local gossip mill. We were a family, and we'd stay that way until the day I died. I'd make damn sure of it.

"You realize I'm pregnant, not helpless, right?"

I lifted Emery into the passenger seat of my truck, the need to get her home strong enough to make my hands shake. "You realize I like doing things for you and am not going to stop that, right?"

"John—"

"Just one more…" I hopped up on the running board and stretched across her, reaching to secure her seat belt around her. "There. Done. Let's go home."

Emery didn't look happy when I slipped into the driver's seat. In fact, she almost looked a little pissed.

I held my tongue as we headed for the parking lot exit. There was only one way out, which meant a bit of a backup. That was fine. Gave me time to figure out why Emery looked so cross.

I reached for her hand, bringing it to my lips for a kiss to her palm. "What's going on, sweet girl?"

"You're being excessive. The cracker delivery in the middle of Kate's speech with my *boss* sitting right next to me? And now actually picking me up and lifting me into the truck? Ridiculous."

"That's nowhere near excessive."

"I should be nothing but irritated with you." She pulled her hand away, turning her face toward her window.

Well, shit. "Should be…but hopefully aren't?"

She huffed, still with her back to me. I inched my way toward the road, thinking over my options. I could pull over and make her talk to me. That might not end well. I could ignore the elephant in the room—well, cab of my truck—but that might piss her off even more. Directness was my only choice.

"Look. I know I can be overbearing sometimes—"

"Understatement."

I clenched my jaw and strangled the steering wheel. "Emery, I like taking care of you."

"I know you do, but I'm perfectly capable of taking care of myself. Just because I'm pregnant with our daughter doesn't mean I forgot how to do so."

I was going to break a tooth from all the clenching. "No, probably not usually. But this time—"

"This time, I was fine. You didn't even give me the chance to take care of myself."

This woman could frustrate me like no other. "Really? Because you looked pale up on that stage. That's why I brought you crackers and water. I didn't want you puking all over your boss's shoes in front of half the town."

"I have ginger candies tucked into my purse for exactly that reason. See? Taking care of myself. And that doesn't excuse your picking me up. What, my legs suddenly don't work?"

Temper. Snapped. "I like touching you, okay? Fuck, baby. I miss you when we're not together. I'd never let you go, never take my hands off your body if staying connected was at all feasible. You're carrying my baby in that hot little body of yours, and I want to touch you and make sure you're real and safe all the fucking time. Is that such a bad thing?"

She finally settled back in her seat, shooting me a look that could only be described as mischievous. Something that almost had me worried. What had my girl been up to? She didn't let me out of my misery, though. My temper simmered low and hot as I finally made it to the road and turned toward home. In fact, we were halfway there before Emery even said another word.

"Hey, John?"

"What?"

"Would you call that a fight?"

I grunted. "We were arguing a bit for sure. Baby, I know—"

"If it was just arguing and not fighting, do we still get to have make-up sex?"

Aw, fuck. I was hard in a matter of seconds, practically leaking for her before I could even get the words in my head in order. Make-up sex? Yes. Definitely. Except…

"You haven't eaten lunch." But the gravel in my tone and the obscene bulge in my pants gave me away. Emery had to have noticed. She leaned closer, running her fingers up my thigh. Teasing my hard cock through my jeans.

"You can feed me all you want…after."

I grabbed her hand and pressed down on my cock, wanting more pressure. Needing to feel her skin on mine. How could I say no?

"Once we get home—"

"I don't want to wait until we get home. I want to go to our spot."

Our spot. The one where she'd ridden me twice after our first—and only—real fight. The one we'd gone back to for a picnic or two that had turned into rolling around on top of the picnic blanket. The one where I'd proposed to her during a full moon that had made her look like an angel. The woman knew how to press my buttons.

"You're killing me, Em."

She tugged my zipper down and finally wrapped that soft, hot little hand of hers around my erection. "Now, don't go dying on me. I have plans for you right now."

I pressed my foot harder on the gas pedal, flying down the lakefront road. Emery didn't let up her teasing, didn't even pause. She stroked me from root to tip, looking awfully calm and slightly proud of herself as I groaned and rocked into her hand. The little hellion. I only slowed down when we reached the turnoff for the wooded road. By then, her smile had me convinced I'd been duped in the best way possible.

"You planned this, didn't you?"

She bit her lip, holding back a grin. "Who, me?"

When I reached the edge of the dirt road that led to the lake, I slammed on the brakes, threw the truck into park, and released my seat belt. Emery wanted to play? I was down.

"You definitely planned this." I slid into the middle seat before pulling her onto my lap. Her giggle as I lifted her over my thighs about made my heart explode. "You wanted to ride my cock, so you staged our little argument."

Emery rocked against me, staring down with eyes filled with lust. "Maybe. Are you mad?"

Mad for her, mad about her, madly in love… always. Mad at her…never. "I should take you home, bend you over the couch, and spank this little ass."

"And that's supposed to be a punishment?"

"Fuck, Emery." I yanked her down, kissing her deep as I started searching for a zipper to her skirt. One that wasn't there. "How do I get this thing off you?"

She grinned and tugged the tight fabric up her legs. "It stretches."

"Well, hallelujah for that." I brought her mouth back to mine, kissing her softer this time. Slower. I wanted to savor the moment—my angel in my arms, writhing on my lap, teasing my cock with her cloth-covered pussy. Wanting me. "Love you, sweet girl."

Skirt up, Emery moved her panties to the side and lined us up so I could thrust inside, making us both groan. "I love you too, John."

I gripped her hips, supporting her as she began to rock. As she started to chase that crest I knew she needed. "Ride me, baby. Make yourself come on my cock. I've got you."

And I did. I always would. No matter what came barreling into our path or where we ended up, Emery was mine. We'd have our family together, and we'd cherish every moment possible, knowing how short life could be.

We were only getting started.

about the author

London Hale is the combined pen name of writing besties Ellis Leigh and Brighton Walsh. Between them, they've published more than thirty books in the contemporary romance, paranormal romance, and romantic suspense genres. Ellis is a *USA Today* bestselling author who loves coffee, thinks green Skittles are the best, and prefers to stay in every weekend. Brighton is multi-published with Berkley, St. Martin's Press, and Carina Press. She hates coffee, thinks green Skittles are the work of the devil, and has never heard of a party she didn't want to attend. Don't ask how they became such good friends or work so well together—they still haven't figured it out themselves.

www.londonhale.com